Clarice Bean

Think Like An Elf

HarperCollins *Children's Books*

Lauren Child

The Twelve Days of Christmas

Allegretto

On the first day of Christ-mas my true love sent to me A

part-ridge— in a pear tree. On the se-cond day of Christ-mas my

true love sent to me Two tur-tle doves and a part-ridge— in a pear

tree. On the third day of Christ-mas my true love sent to me

Three French— hens, two tur-tle doves and a part-ridge— in a pear

tree. On the fourth day of Christ-mas my true love sent to me

Four call-ing birds, three French— hens, two tur-tles doves and a part - ridge__ in a pear tree. On the fifth day of Christ - mas my

true love sent to me five gold__ rings, Four call - ing birds,

three French__ hens, two tur - tle doves and a part - ridge__ in a pear

tree. On the sixth day of Christ - mas my true love sent to me

Six geese a - lay - ing, five gold__ rings, Four call - ing birds,

three French__ hens, two tur - tle doves and a part - ridge__ in a pear

tree. On the seventh day of Christ - mas my true love sent to me . . .

The Beginning of Things

ONE THING WE ALL AGREE ON IN OUR
house is that we like looking forward
to Christmas.

My favourite song for this time of the year is
'The Twelve Days of Christmas'.
I'm not sure exactly what it is about.
I used to think it was Christmas shopping,
but Betty Moody says it's to do with
the twelve days AFTER Christmas.

But why would someone give you
ALL those presents when it is all OVER?

And why would they give you
so many BIRDS?

It might be to do with
the Christmas sales
but Betty says they
DIDN'T have sales
in the
olden days.

When Christmas begins
I sing
'*The Twelve Days of Christmas*'
ALL THE TIME
but I tend not to know
what comes AFTER
the seven swans
are swimming.

7

Talking of seven, we are also seven in our family.
Which is:

my mum and my dad,

my older brother, Kurt,

my older sister, Marcie,

Me, Clarice Bean,

my grandad, who is an
actual live-in older relative,

and my younger brother,
Minal Cricket.

If we were like those
families in the books,
we would look like THIS,

all nicely sitting down, listening to each other
in a smiling way – like you see
on the Christmas cards.

But usually, actually, we look more like THIS . . .

which is talking
or
NOT talking
all at the same time
from different
rooms.

I live on Navarino Street,
number 7, and I know LOTS
of the people in our road.
At Christmastime there is
more helloing
and this is because of the
Christmas spirit.

Christmas cannot be Christmas
without the Christmas spirit
so it is IMPORTANT to
keep an eye on it and
NOT let it float away.

Christmas is Coming the Goose is Getting Fat

YOU CAN TELL WHEN IT'S GETTING TO BE Christmas because Mum gets out the Christmas-elf tea towels. We have three of them although we used to have four. Granny sent them to us – they are from New York and along the bottom in embroidery writing they say, 'Think Like Elves'. We have special Christmas water glasses too, which have reindeers leaping up the sides. They are very old. No one must break them because they are heirlooms of the family and very much the spirit of Christmas.

Every year Dad says, 'We drank from these glasses when I was a SMALL child and NOT one of them has ever been dropped.'

This makes me very actually nervous.

There are only six so not quite enough to go round but Grandad says he's happy with a less valuable water glass as he suffers from the collywobbles, which basically means he is liable to drop a glass at any moment.

The other thing which usually happens is that we all tend to bake ginger biscuits, which are decorated with icing. They are sort of chewy and NOT necessarily that nice unless you are in the mood. But I don't mind a not-that-nice biscuit because it is another sign that

Christmas
is
coming.

Something you may also notice is they send you electricity bills with holly printed on the envelope, and cards from people who you can't remember who they are.

If I come downstairs to hear Mum saying,
'Who are Beryl and Terrance?'

and Dad saying,
'I haven't even a clue,'

then
I know
that

Christmas

has

begun.

Actually we never know who
Beryl and Terrance are.

I'm beginning to wonder if
they even know us.

Also we don't know who

J and P and W (Farrell) are,

even though they always write in the card

'really enjoyed bumping into you
this summer'

or

'W is doing really well with
his clarinet'.

Once the Christmas cards begin to arrive,
we arrange them on the kitchen table
and Mum always says,

'It's so lovely to think of all these people
from all these far-off places taking the trouble
to write and send us good cheer.'

And then when more come through the letterbox
we line them up along the living-room shelves
and then along the kitchen shelves
and Mum says,
'Look at that – the spirit of Christmas!'

And then when even more come
we crowd them on the window ledges
and always a few of them fall into
the washing-up.
And Mum says, 'These cards are a
blimming nuisance.'
But really there is nowhere else to
put them so it is unavoidable that
some end up in the sink.

We used to peg
them up on a string
across the kitchen but
then one year some of
them decided to fall into
the stir-fry and they got
set on fire, and it could have
been much worse if Kurt
hadn't thrown a dampened
cloth over the wok.

Think Like Elv

My Uncle Ted, who is
in the fire brigade, told us
our Christmas cards were
a FIRE HAZARD
waiting to happen.
He was right, and we were
lucky not to lose more than the
Christmas-elf tea towel.
He said, 'You just CANNOT
have Christmas cards
dangling
over naked flames.
What were
you thinking?'
Everyone looked sheepish.
So now there is a strict law in
our house about cards – when
too many arrive through the
letterbox all the ugly ones
get shuffled into
the recycling.

18

I say, 'Mum, you do know you are throwing
people's Christmas spirit in the actual dustbin?'
And Mum whispers,
        'Whatever you do, don't tell anyone!'

★ ★ ★

The shops will try to make you believe
Christmas is arriving in October,
but Mum says you must ignore them.
She says,

        'Could they just let me carve
                my pumpkin, for goodness' sake!
        We haven't even had Halloween yet!'

Some people even send their cards in November,
which is too early since Christmas can't really
begin until the 1st of December.
December the 1st is when you can start opening
        the TINY DOORS on the Advent calendar
                        and from then on . . .

Mind you, this year we don't even have an Advent calendar because Mum decided we would instead have an **Advent candle**, which is basically a candle with numbers up it.
She said,
'It will **bring** more **togetherness** to our **home** because we will **light it every evening** as a **family** during supper.'
We have to burn it down **one notch** at a time and then *blow* it out, which is **not** as interesting as opening a TINY DOOR.
But Granny told me you can use it to make a **Christmas wish** every time you blow it out, which means **twenty-four** wishes. I'm going to wish for **snow** and if I do it **twenty-four** times in a row it will probably work even though Dad says the weather people say there's **not** even a **smidge** of a **chance** this year.
Grandad says, 'It's going to be *blowing* a gale and it's going to be **nothing** but gales.'
Grandad knows about **weather** because he was **brought up** with it.

21

Most people have those Advent calendars with chocolate animals to surprise you, but these have been banned in our house because some people kept eating other actual people's animals and this led to complaints. Because I'm missing having a true Advent calendar made of paper, I've made my own one and I've drawn little pictures for each day. I'm trying to surprise myself by forgetting what is behind the TINY DOORS . . .

So far I have NOT been fooled.

★ ★ ★

Usually we have Christmas at home.
I think this is because Mum hates packing and Dad says it is too much effort to get seven people and a dog in a car all at the same time.
This year Mum says she fancies a quietish Christmas where nothing much happens. She says, 'Let's just be the seven of us.'

But some of us prefer things to be more than seven, so I am a bit disappointed by this announcement. You see, I really like the Christmases when LOTS of people come, and when LOTS of people stay.
I thought we ALL did but it turns out Mum and Dad are feeling exhausted by the thought of it. I'm not sure how you can be exhausted by a thought, but this seems to be something which happens to you when you get older.
I know this because when Marcie asks,
'Why can't everyone come?'
Mum says, 'Just thinking about it . . .'
She doesn't even finish her sentence – she just flumps down on the chair.
And Dad shakes his head and says, 'Exactly.'
And Mum says, 'I feel exhausted already.'
Kurt says, 'But it's no fun if everyone isn't here.'
Everyone is surprised by this because Kurt normally doesn't bother with fun. He just spends all his time in his room with headphones on.
Marcie says, 'It will just be totally BORING if it's only us.'
Minal says, 'Yes, let's have everyone!'

Dad says, 'If you four are prepared
to do all the shopping and all the
cooking, then fine – ask as
many people as you like.'

I say,
'Thanks, we will.'

Marcie and Kurt stomp off to their rooms
and Minal says,

'Don't look at me – I'm standing on my head.'

Which, by the way, he is NOT.

My brother CAN'T do headstands.

I say, 'OK, I will do everything.'

Dad says, 'I'll write you out a shopping list.'

Mum says, 'The recipe books are on the shelf
next to the fridge.'

Dad says, 'How many people are you thinking of inviting?'

I say, 'Twelve.'

I say twelve because I've got the song of *'The Twelve Days of Christmas'* stuck in my brain. It's like there are people singing it inside my actual head and I can't STOP them.

Mum says, 'So twelve plus the seven of us makes nineteen in all. How many potatoes will you need to cook, I wonder?'

Dad says, 'At least four per person – are you inviting Uncle Ted?'

I say, 'Of course – he is the MAIN one.'

Dad says, 'Well, Ted always eats extra and it's nice to have some left over for Boxing Day . . . so better make it six each plus a few for the pot.'

I can't even work out what 19 x 6 is – let alone how much a few for the pot comes to. I am busy trying to do the times-ing but then Dad says,

'One hundred and fourteen potatoes plus about six more!'

I say, 'How am I going to peel
one hundred and fourteen potatoes
plus six more?'
Mum says, 'You'll just have to get up early.'
Dad says, 'I suggest five a.m.'
I'm not really an early rising sort of person, and
I go up to my room feeling strangely tired. I'm
beginning to understand how a thought can
actually wear you out since just thinking about
counting out one hundred and fourteen plus six
potatoes has made me need to lie down.
If I'm this tired just thinking about peeling
potatoes, then how will I feel after I have actually
done them? I expect I won't have the energy to
talk or cook a turkey or maybe even to watch telly.
I decide it's useless to try to make Christmas more
than seven.

Slowly I am feeling the Christmas spirit

evaporating

out   of

me.

TWO

Goodwill to all Peoplekind

IN THE MIDDLE OF THE NIGHT AT 5AM while I am still awake worrying about the evaporating Christmas spirit, I begin to see how it is more important than ever to spread goodwill to all peoplekind, since we won't now be peeling potatoes for them.

If we are not going to be sharing our Christmas spirit on the actual day of Christmas, then at least I can post some through the letterbox.

I'm going to need a LOT more cards than usual.

I always make my own cards. Mum says it is more personal this way and 'so much better than just going to the shop and buying them off the rack'. This is very easy for her to say because she is NOT the one working herself down to the fingers.

Normally I tend to leave the making to the last minute because there is so much else to do. This can have a benefit because you can see who sent you a card, and you can see who DIDN'T, which means you don't have to find yourself sending cards to people who don't bother sending one to you. Although when I explained this to Mum she said that strictly speaking this is NOT in the Christmas spirit.

She told me, 'You should post cards to anyone and everyone – it doesn't matter if you don't get one back.'

This must be what Beryl and Terrance have decided because we never send them one back – we can't! We don't know their address!

I have decided to be influenced by Beryl and Terrance and I'm going to make cards for ALL the neighbours in our street even if I don't know them. I will also send one to the corner shop, one to the post-office-convenient store, one to the vegetarian organic shop which is Eggplant and maybe also the vet's because Dad says we need to keep in with them.

Mum says generosity can have a good effect on bad relationships so I will also make cards for people who don't like me.

This means Mrs Stampney.

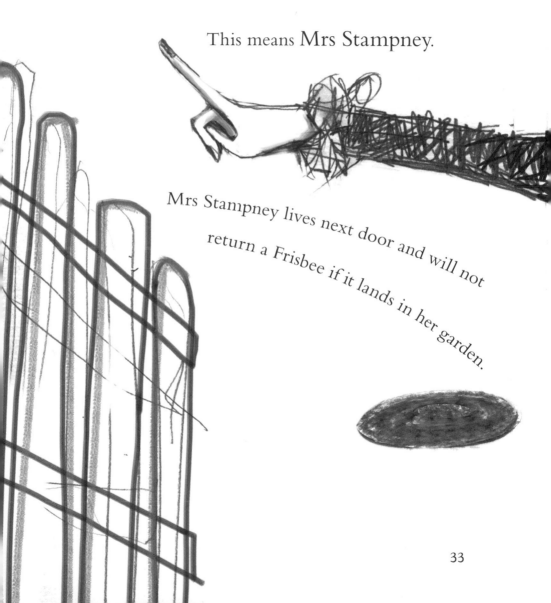

Mrs Stampney lives next door and will not return a Frisbee if it lands in her garden.

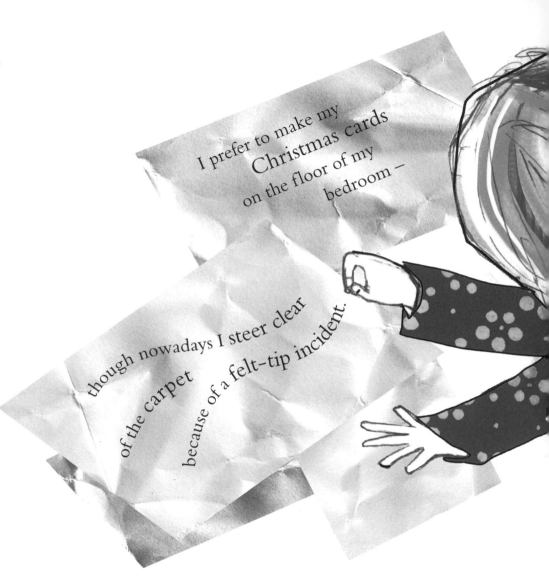

I prefer to make my
Christmas cards
on the floor of my
bedroom –

though nowadays I steer clear
of the carpet
because of a felt-tip incident.

I used to like drawing a shape in glue and
pouring glitter all over it – glitter makes
everything instantly better than it was.

But my
brother Kurt
says

glitter is a **HAZARD** to fish.

He says it gets into the oceans and causes
problems and you WOULDN'T believe
how many fish are eating glitter these days.

You wouldn't think something so SMALL could cause problems to something so big, i.e. the sea.

But Kurt is an environmentalist and he knows about these things.

So now I'm trying to come up with other ways of creating the Christmas effect without making fish eat glitter.

The question is I need a good idea. I've been STRETCHING my brain to think how I can make cards out of something that causes less upset in the ocean. It needs to be something which doesn't cost any money, so it has to be something I've already got.

Minal says, 'Why don't you use macaroni?'

That's his answer to EVERYTHING and he has got everyone to buy tonnes of it, and now Mum says he's going to have to make a LOT more jewellery or we'll never get through it.

I say, 'I'm not going to stick old dried-up food on my cards, thank you very much.'

Kurt says, 'Why don't you recycle stuff instead of using the planet's valuable resources?

It's all going to end up in the bin anyway.'

And then suddenly a good idea pops into my head, the way it sometimes does when you are utterly desperate.

I will rescue the Christmas spirit from the dustbin where Mum has chucked it and

cut up all the ugly cards and turn them into newly reinvented ones.

It works like a charm and once they are all

snipped into pieces

and stuck down in different directions they look much nicer and also very cheerful.

Since I am in a making-things frame of mind I also make Granny a Christmas present, which is a TINY-USEFUL-THINGS BAG — it was meant to be for lavender except when it came to it I didn't have any.

A good tip to remember when making your gifts is to check you have the vital pieces of ingredients. If not, you must adapt your ambition, which is what I have done.

Once I've finished I hand it to Mum because she is busy parcelling up other presents for Granny, who lives in New York. We have to send them out early because they are travelling a very long way so it takes a while. Minal has made Granny his usual macaroni necklace.

Dad says it doesn't matter that it is a repeated gift because Granny wore her last macaroni necklace in a rainstorm and it went a bit soft.

Mum is really impressed with my TINY-USEFUL-THINGS BAG and she loves the recycled ugly Christmas cards, but whispers, 'Just try NOT to mail them back to their original senders.'

My recycling has inspired her to do some recycling of her own and at the same time do a good deed for others and clear out some clobber before Christmas. She has had a sort-out and is collecting our old jumpers and cardies – the ones that have gone into strange shapes and the ones that have holes too big to easily mend without knitting a whole entire sleeve. She is sending them on to Mr Felixstow's knitwear appeal. Mr Felixstow does something with the wool and this turns into money for a good cause.

He wrote to us on a leaflet that came through the door asking for help from strangers. Mum looked it up on the computer and it turns out there's a LOT you can do with old knitted things if you know how.

I wish I knew how because she is giving Mr Felixstow a couple of my favourite cardigans and I'm sorry to see them go.

Dad says, 'I hope you DIDN'T put my Christmas-elf sweater in there.'

And Mum says, 'Of course not.'

But I can tell she is lying because she pretends to sneeze – she always pretends to sneeze when she is telling a WHOPPER.

★ ★ ★

While Mum and I are doing good deeds at home,
Dad and Marcie go off to help Uncle Ted with
his move to a much SMALLER place.
He is now going to be living with his girlfriend.
She is called JoJo and she has black hair
which is sometimes red
and cut at a SLANT.

She is training to do lighting for the theatre,
but at the moment is working at the old-people's
centre being the maintenance fixer.
Uncle Ted and JoJo need to move into their flat in
time for Christmas.
Mum says, 'They want to spend the day together
in their new home, just the TWO of them.'
I don't know why they would want that, but
everyone's being a bit strange this year and has
let the Christmas spirit dri f t.
Dad and Marcie are gone ages and they come back
from Uncle Ted's at almost teatime, very tired
and with LOTS more BOXES of clobber,
more than Mum just got rid of.

Dad says the flat is very SMALL indeed and Ted
and JoJo have had to go MINIMALIST, which
means no unneeded items, i.e. all their stuff is
moving into our shed.
The good news is that we now have a secondary
fridge down the garden.
Marcie says, 'Ted and JoJo's flat looks really cool.'
Mum says, 'I'm very pleased for them.'
Marcie says, 'Why can't we have a
                          MINIMALIST house?'
Mum says, 'We can – we just need to
        find someone who is willing to let us put
                all our clobber in their shed.'
Dad says, 'I doubt if anyone has a shed big
                enough for our clobber.'
That night we have a simple meal of baked beans,
and make-your-own toast if you want it.
I ask Mum if I can eat it on my lap while I watch
the **RUBY REDFORT** series on the telly, but she
points to a notice she has written that says:

NO EATING on the SOFA due to
SPILLAGES and crumbs.

Mum says she is also concerned that there might be a possible mouse on the loose. She says, 'Cement keeps barking at something and I can only think it is a TINY visitor.'

Minal says, 'He's NOT barking at a mouse – he's barking at the FOX.'

My brother Minal Cricket is obsessed about foxes since he was given this book about a fox who comes into people's houses when they aren't looking and eats their dinner and finally the Christmas turkey.

Mum says it's the first book that has really caught his imagination.

Minal talks about it non-non-stop and he thinks it's the most fascinating idea EVER written, though of course it ISN'T.

I understand how you can be so caught up in a book that it almost becomes true. It's like with me and **RUBY REDFORT**. Sometimes I can't help thinking she's real and I often wish I could go and live in Twinford, which is where Ruby is from. If you don't know who Ruby Redfort is, you should, because she is a book character who is also a schoolkid secret agent and the stories are really gripping and NOT for drips. There are at least about fifty-two books and all of them get you on the edge of your seat.

Eating at the table instead of on the sofa does remind me that we almost forgot to light the Advent candle – it is very hard to remember this new habit. I make sure I get to blow it out so I can wish for snow, and as soon as I have I rush to switch the telly on. I am desperate of course to watch because it is the **RUBY REDFORT CHRISTMAS SPECIAL**: PART ONE.

Unfortunately I've already missed the beginning credits with the FLY LOGO buzzing you into Twinford. The fly is important because this is the symbol for the SECRET AGENCY called **SPECTRUM** where Ruby Redfort works. The episode begins with Mrs Redfort bringing home a huge Christmas tree – of course it is snowing because in Ruby Redfort's life everything turns out the way it's meant to. The episode ends on a cliffhanger where Ruby gets told she must jump out of a helicopter and ski to a secret location.

My evening ends with
Mum telling me to
get off the sofa
and hop up
to bed.

THREE

Glad Tidings of Great Joy

ONE OF THE SECOND FIRST THINGS
you need to do when you are getting ready for
Christmas is make a list of all the things you
will need to buy for your dearest ones and your
younger brother. Then you need to look in your
piggy bank – mine is a toadstool – and discover
that you are probably going to have to hand-make
nearly all your gifts because the price of things
is NOT covered by your pocket money.
Especially when you are hoping to spend more
than you actually have on a present for your
friend Betty Moody.

The thing I'm wanting to buy her is this:
THE RUBY REDFORT FLY READER BOOK LIGHT.
The light is a fly attached to a bendy thing and it clips on to your book when you want to read in the dark and it's mail order only.

I need to order it soon or it WON'T arrive in time.

It is utterly OUT of my price range.

It's easy to shop for Betty Moody, but it is hard to think of things that everyone else might like. Especially things that you can actually make for not too much money.

In the end I think it will come down to fudge.

These are the people on my list:

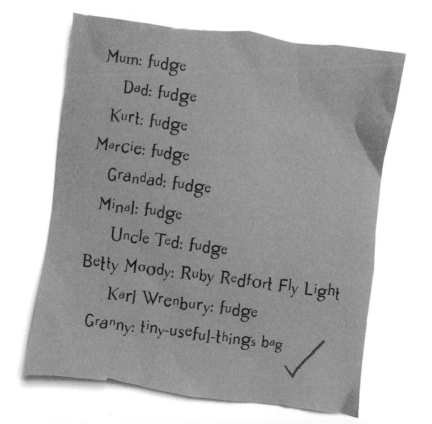

Mum: fudge
Dad: fudge
Kurt: fudge
Marcie: fudge
Grandad: fudge
Minal: fudge
Uncle Ted: fudge
Betty Moody: Ruby Redfort Fly Light
Karl Wrenbury: fudge
Granny: tiny-useful-things bag ✓

I have also made a list
of the things I'd like
for Christmas
        and this is it:

A piano

Piano music

A pair of roller-skates

A Ruby Redfort long-distance
secret-agent walkie-talkie

A fish tank

Some fish

Some fish food

Snow

I have added snow because
I don't know if the Advent candle is
up to it – the granting wishes, I mean.
I'm not sure if this is an up-the-chimney for
Father Christmas list or a list for Mum and Dad.
Sometimes I think that maybe my mum and dad
have taken over from Father Christmas. I've asked
about this, but they always say it ISN'T true. But
I'm puzzling about why Father Christmas and my
mum and dad would all use the same wrapping
paper. I mean, I'm not sure why Father Christmas
would bother to get his wrapping paper from the
post-office-convenient store on Park Road if he
really does live all the way over in Lapland.

Dad says, 'He probably likes their range,
    and the prices aren't bad.'
But I would have thought Father Christmas would
have his own convenient store. I'm certain it
would be more convenient to buy it from
somewhere near his actual workshop.
I'm still trying to make a decision about this
problem when Mum calls out that Betty is on
the phone.
As you know, Betty Moody is my best friend.
She is in my class – we always sit together.
Betty asks if I'd like to come over and have lunch
at her house. Which I would because I like going
round to the Moodys'. Betty calls her mum and
dad by their first names and if anyone ever calls
them Mr and Mrs Moody they always say,
'Call me Cecil,' or, 'Call me Mol.'
They are very friendly people.
Because I don't want to waste any time not being
at Betty's, I start madly stuffing my cards into their
envelopes. This is tricky because I didn't think of
what size the envelope would be when I made the
cards, so it is a tight squeeze and some folding over.

I want to post my neighbourhood cards on the
way to the Moodys' as this is sensible doubling-up,
which is known as multitasking. It is very
wise to multitask at Christmas because there
is SO much to do.
Mum says, 'Goodness me, you have certainly
made a LOT of cards. Who are they all for?'
I explain that most of them are for the people
in our street.
I say, 'The ones I don't know I have just
written on the envelope, "for the householder",
because I have seen this done with some of
    our letters from the council
            and the junk mail people do it too.'
Dad says, 'This might look a bit impersonal.'
I can see what he means. Mum agrees.
She says, 'It's NOT very Christmassy.'
Marcie says, 'They'll probably put it in the bin.'
So we quickly cross this out and instead I add
in felt tip: To my neighbours
Dad says, 'Much more friendly!'
        It's true – this is much more
                in the style of Christmas.

Inside the cards I have written:

> Dear neighbour,
> Wishing you glad tidings of joy from
> a well-wisher in your neighbourhood.
> Clarice Bean

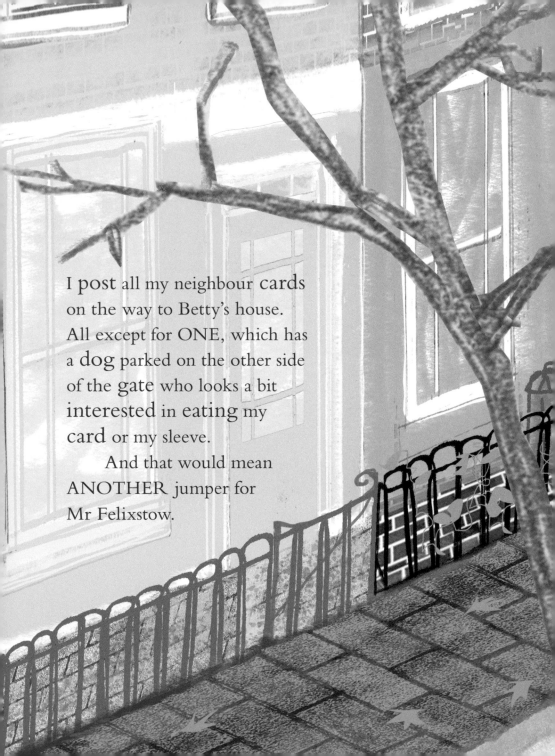

I post all my neighbour cards
on the way to Betty's house.
All except for ONE, which has
a dog parked on the other side
of the gate who looks a bit
interested in eating my
card or my sleeve.

And that would mean
ANOTHER jumper for
Mr Felixstow.

While I am walking, I think
about my Father Christmas list
and I can't help wondering HOW he is
going to FIT a piano in a stocking.

It doesn't take long to get to the Moodys' house
because they are more or less round the corner
just five or so streets away.
The Moodys' house is upside down,*
the same as Ruby Redfort's, but it doesn't
have a laundry chute.
When I get there I ring the doorbell, which
makes a pipe-ish sound because it is unusual
and not the normal kind of doorbell and possibly
from the Far East. Betty answers in socks.
No shoes are worn in the Moodys' home.
We go upstairs to the kitchen, and call-me-Cecil
says, 'Hello, Clarice Bean.
You are just in time for lunch!'
Call-me-Mol says,
'We are having macrobiotic soup.'
I do not know if this is a vegetable or a flavour,
but it sounds interesting to me.
The Moodys always eat things that you've
never heard of.

---

* An upside-down house is one where the bedrooms are on
the ground floor and the kitchen and living room are above.

Mol says, 'Clarice, do you like daikon, pickled?'
And I don't know because I have no idea what
it is even when it ISN'T pickled.
But I say, 'Yes,' because it's important
to expand what you eat.

It turns out
that it tastes
of what most things do
when they are
pickled,
which is mainly
vinegar.

The Moodys want Betty to see Japan so they are going there for Christmas.

I wish my mum and dad wanted me to see Japan. They are travelling there along with Betty's much older brother, Zack, to visit his girlfriend and her family who are, in fact, Japanese.

It is a shame for me because it means I will not see Betty for most of the Christmas holidays.

Usually we even see each other on the actual Christmas Day but this year we will be sadly separated and not together. However, on the plus side Betty said she will purchase me some of those Japanese big-toe socks that you can wear with flip-flops.

These kinds of socks are very traditional in Japan. I have always wanted some.

Mol says, 'It will be a different sort of Christmas.' Which is true because Betty won't even arrive in Japan until Christmas Day in the morning so Christmas for her will start by NOT being anywhere at all.

Mol says,
    'This will be
interesting,'

        and Betty says,
            'And also fun.'

And I say how I couldn't agree
more because the Moodys will
be surrounded by hundreds of
travelling people and Christmas is
all about being with people. And
then I tell Mol how my mum and
dad have reduced Christmas to
seven, and how disappointed I
feel, 'Because that is almost hardly
anyone! It makes me feel like
Christmas has utterly fallen apart
before it has started.'
Mol looks out of the window like
she is trying to see something,
but I think it's in her head, the
something she's trying to find.
And then she says,

'As Marilyn Monroe once said, "Sometimes **good things fall apart** so **better things** can fall **together**."'

Marilyn Monroe is a famous film star from the olden days and me and Grandad like watching her films when it's a damp afternoon. Usually they're in black and white.

Mol says,

'So **my advice** would be, focus on what's **good** and **Christmas** may well **surprise** you.'

Mol has a habit of saying things in a way that makes you think she knows something you don't know, so when she says this I feel strangely better. But of course there's another problem.

I say, 'That's the other problem.

I'm trying to focus on making things good but I'm a bit stuck with my presents because it turns out my toadstool doesn't have that much money in it, so I'm going to be making something homemade which is fudge.'

Cecil says,

'Oh, I love homemade fudge.'

And I say, 'That's why it's a good idea because *everyone* loves fudge. I am buying all the ingredients myself because otherwise it would feel more like a present from the larder than from me.'

Mol says,

'That's very thoughtful of you, Clarice Bean.'

I say, 'Plus we don't have condensed milk or vanilla essence or the right kind of butter and also there isn't much sugar in the jar and these are the essentially vital ingredients.'

Cecil says, 'I see the problem.'

Betty says, 'What will you put the fudge in?'
And I say, 'That's the other problem.

Gift boxes, it turns out, are much more expensive than the gift to go in them.'
Mol says, 'This is so often true.'
Then she thinks a bit and suddenly says,
'I might have the perfect idea for you.'
And she does.

It involves cutting paper into slices and weaving it back together and like magic you have a TINY basket in the shape of a heart, which is also a tree decoration.
It looks tricky but it is simple and Betty and me make a zillion of them, or at least eighteen even though I don't need that many. While we work we are chatting about other things, mainly to do with fish.
After that me and Betty go and sit in her room on beanbags and we talk about the **RUBY REDFORT LONG-DISTANCE WALKIE-TALKIES** we both want, and I tell her all about my list. And how I am wondering why Mum and Dad always say that

Christmas lists must be posted up the chimney on Christmas Eve because you see it doesn't leave much time for Father Christmas to shop.

Betty says, 'What are your parents talking about? You CAN'T leave your list until Christmas Eve. You have to post it much earlier than that.'

And I say, 'I know. It's one thing finding a piano at the last minute because I expect he keeps those in stock but those **RUBY REDFORT WALKIE-TALKIES** are very popular and I worry they will have all sold out if he leaves it so late.'

Betty says, 'Also chimneys are very unreliable. You must use an actual post box and a first-class stamp. No one uses chimneys these days.'

I say, 'This is probably the whole reason why I NEVER get what I ask for.'

She says, 'Exactly. He needs more warning.'

And I say, 'I wonder why my mum and dad don't want him to have more warning?'

And Betty says, 'It's very strange. It's almost as if maybe they DON'T want you to have a piano or a fish tank.'

I say, 'I know!'

Betty says I might as well rub out the bit asking for
snow because Father Christmas ISN'T in charge
of the weather, which makes me wonder who is.
Then I tell Betty my other worry, which I have
to whisper in case Father Christmas can hear.

I say, 'Sometimes I wonder, what if

you-know-who is NOT in actually fact true.'

Betty looks confused so I whisper,

'Am I believing in NOTHING?'

Betty says, 'What makes you wonder that?'
And I say, 'Because I have never seen him.'
Betty says, 'But you're not MEANT to see him?'
I say, 'But I have never even

heard a whispering elf.'

And Betty says, 'But elves are very quiet.
They are trained to NOT make a sound.' Then
she says, 'Just because you CAN'T see something
or hear something DOESN'T mean it isn't there.'
And this is true because think of a i r.

Betty says, 'You don't have to stop believing in
Father Christmas. You just need a back-up plan.'

I never get to hear what the back-up plan is because before Betty can actually tell me there is the sound of the doorbell pipes and there is my dad on the doorstep.

So I'm left in suspense as to what the back-up plan might be. It's the kind of thing that happens to Ruby Redfort all the time but rarely happens so much in real life.

★ ★ ★

When Dad and I get home Minal is still going on about a fox in the garden but every time we look there isn't one. Foxes is all my brother can talk about if he's not going on about macaroni.

Dad is looking in the fridge and he says,

'Where is that nice cheese I bought?'

Minal says, 'The fox ate it.'

Dad is quite cross about this.

He says, 'Foxes DON'T even eat cheese.'

Minal says, 'This one does.'

Dad says, 'It's been a very tiring day, and I'm too exhausted to argue or discuss the problem of

cheese-eating foxes.
Let's just eat biscuits
on the sofa.'
I am about to point out
the notice Mum
wrote asking us
NOT to eat
biscuits on the
sofa due to crumbs
and mice but Dad
DOESN'T look in
the mood for it.

NO EATING
on the SOFA
due to SPILLAGES
and crumbs.

★ ★ ★

When I pop in to say goodnight to Grandad
I hear his radio say,

'Strong winds still predicted

which luckily reminds me to go and light the
Advent candle so I can wish against wind and
make it snow. Of course I can only blow it out
when it has burned down to the right number,
which means I'm still up when Mum gets home,
so I am in hot water for NOT being in bed.
I lie there thinking about the Moodys and all the
things we talked about and what call-me-Mol
said about good things falling apart so better
things can fall together.
I gradually drift off with this thought in my head
and I am sure I will dream of snow
                    and pianos
                            and socks with toes.

But actually I dream of foxes
   sitting in the kitchen eating
   our Christmas dinner.

for Christmas,

FOUR

Hark
Hear the Bells

DESPITE THE FOX IN MY DREAMS, I WAKE
up actually in an exceptionordinarily happy mood.
Because, you see, my Christmas hopes are
much less squashed since I saw Betty and Cecil
and Mol.

That's the thing about the Moodys —
they always make you feel hopeful.

I'm not really a schoolish person normally but I'm
looking forward to today because it's the last day
of it before the holidays.

My main problem with school is Mrs Wilberton.
She is my teacher and I really wish she was
Mrs Nesbit.

The reason I do not get on with Mrs Wilberton is because I tend to be in her bad books.

You see I am NOT a good speller or a good dividerer, and unfortunately these are two things which Mrs Wilberton thinks are more important than life itself. If you can't spell things the way the dictionaries want to spell things, or you can't divide 145 by 17, then Mrs Wilberton will NOT be your biggest admirer.

Anyway, today is different because nothing needs to be spelled or divided – it just has to be decorated, and that's what I'm good at.

There are no worries, and you just have to watch a Christmas film while you eat a Christmas biscuit on the gym mats.

I wish school could always be doing this.

I am out of bed before my alarm clock has even told me to wake up. I remember what call-me-Mol said yesterday about focusing on the good things. And I wonder if I can make the good things more by also *doing* good things.

So while I am brushing my teeth I clean the washbasin. It's easy to do with one hand –

you just slide the soap around and *swish it* with a flannel.

I use Kurt's because he never does.

I come
downstairs
in my
usual
way,

which is with a jumper half over my head.
On school days I tend to get dressed on the move
so I'm not late. I'm mostly always late.
When I have managed to poke my head
through I am surprised to see Betty Moody is
on the doormat.
This is very unusual because she never comes
over before school since I am not on the way.
I say, 'Wotcha, Betty, how did you get there?'
She says, 'It's a long story,' because that's exactly
what Ruby Redfort's friend Clancy Crew would
say but actually it is quite a short one involving
Minal answering the door to Betty but not
bothering to tell me she is here – instead he has
gone off to eat Sugar Puffs in the kitchen.
  Betty is too polite to just run upstairs to
        my room because it is still quite early
            in the morning and some of us
              are cutting it fine and
                    still in their pyjamas.
                Betty says she has come
                  round with the
                        back-up plan,

which is basically lots of pieces of paper with the same thing written on all of them.

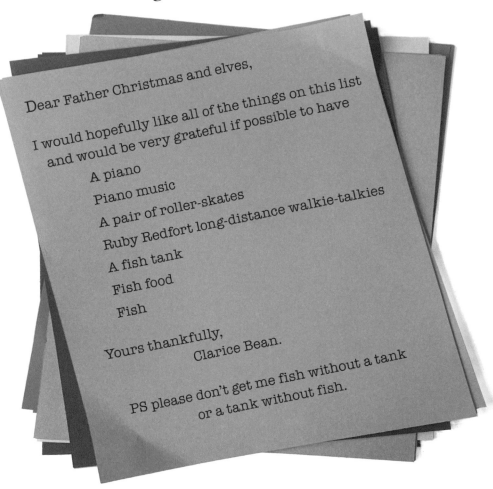

Dear Father Christmas and elves,

I would hopefully like all of the things on this list and would be very grateful if possible to have

    A piano

    Piano music

    A pair of roller-skates

    Ruby Redfort long-distance walkie-talkies

    A fish tank

    Fish food

    Fish

Yours thankfully,
        Clarice Bean.

PS please don't get me fish without a tank or a tank without fish.

Betty says, 'Leave the list lying around so that your mum and dad also see it and have a chance to buy you the piano and everything, just in case Father Christmas is NOT interested and, or, NOT in existence.'

I say, 'What if I end up with two pianos?'

Betty says, 'You can return one and get a credit note.'

I say, 'What's a credit note?'

Betty says, 'It's like a token that you can exchange for something that costs the same amount as the unwanted piano.'

I say, 'In that case I hope I get two pianos.'

Betty says, 'But remember you can only spend it in the musical-instrument shop so you might have to end up choosing a harp or a trumpet since they are unlikely to have much else.'

This doesn't bother me because I have always been interested in owning a harp.

Betty and me find some good places to casually leave my lists so people can accidentally read them. We put one above the bathroom sink taped to the mirror. One is stuck to the TV and one on Mum and Dad's bedroom door and one inside Mum's handbag. These seem the most likely places to

grab people's attention without meaning to.
We also stick one up the chimney just in case
Father Christmas prefers to get his post this way.
You never know.
There is no time for breakfast so I take one of
Kurt's organically made energy bars and a piece
of cheese for flavour, which is exactly what
Ruby Redfort would do in my shoes.

★ ★ ★

This year at school we are having another carol
concert. Mrs Wilberton always announces it
like it is a big surprise and a completely new
invention that she has come up with even though
people have probably been having carol concerts at
their schools for thousands or even millions of
years since the dawn of time.
The thing Mrs Wilberton is trying to teach is
learning to sing in harmony. She says that,
in fact, I, Clarice Bean, do NOT have a
harmonic type of voice and I am
sending everyone else out of tune.

She says I need to 'pipe down considerably'.

I think this is unfair coming from someone who has a voice that is the sound of constant droning. At least my voice can go up and down – she only has one note and it is FLAT. Mrs Wilberton is more excited than usual because our school is singing at the Julia Moggan Concert Hall, which is extremely old and also historical. Mrs Wilberton is very proud of herself but it is actually, in fact, thank you to Betty's dad, because he came up with the idea and organised it. He is a musician and plays in a very important orchestra, which is famous for music.

Lots of people will be there – not just the family ones but people who are actually expecting it to be good.

We have to wear gold or silver capes and some of the parents and people have made these from fabric given by Arnie Singh's mother, who has kindly donated it.

Mum is bringing a group from the old people's centre and Grandad and his friend Peggy will also be coming.

Peggy is Grandad's 'Betty Moody' and she lives not too far from our house so they see each other most days.

Peggy used to be a singer but she says her lungs aren't what they were, although they seem very good to me. She says she will give me some tips on tunefulness. She says it's all in the breathing.

I was hoping I would be given one of the solo–ish parts of '*The Twelve Days of Christmas*' since I've gone to a lot of effort to learn what comes after the seven swans are swimming.

I would even do the eleven or so pipers piping part but Mrs Wilberton has decided to get twelve

other children singing and I am only allowed
to join in with everyone else when my voice will
be drowned out by Robert Granger.

Robert Granger lives over the wall
and is annoying.

* * *

At break I give out all the rest of my Christmas cards to the people in my class including Grace Grapello and Cindy Fisher, which they are both quite surprised about but also pleased. And I can see how Mum is right about how being *generous* to the people you think don't like you can have a good effect. We all have to be outside in the playground even though it is very cold and you can hardly get your fingers to grip a skipping rope – it is important to skip when the temperatures are freezing otherwise you could seize up and perish.

If Ruby Redfort was at our school, she would start a campaign to prevent children being forced to stand in icy conditions. This is what's good about Ruby: she is an activist and won't take cruelty to children for an answer.

Winter is the only time I am just waiting for the school bell to ring and tell me: class has re-begun. You may THAW OUT. Normally I have to defrost before I can even pick up a pencil.

Even though this is finally and actually the last day of school before Christmas, it is *not* the last day of seeing Mrs Wilberton since she will be popping up again at the Christmas concert, so it's not quite a relief of goodbyes.

When we all flurry out of the school gates

Karl Wrenbury is

DRAGGING

his feet along

WITHOUT

cheerfulness.

It turns out he is down in the dumps because his younger brother Alf is home with a flu-ish cold and so cannot be outside. This means Karl cannot do his dog-walking job with his mum because someone has to stay home with Alf and although Jean-next-door will be keeping an eye on things, Karl's mum says she needs Karl to keep an eye on Jean who is often on the phone and NOT paying enough attention to Alf.

Karl's mum is a professional dog walker and walks several dogs all at once. Karl has two dog customers of his own, which is all he can manage until he is eleven and more experienced.

No one understands more about dogs than Mrs Wrenbury and she is teaching Karl everything she knows so he will very soon be an expert.

He has been teaching my grandad about training Cement, and Grandad is at last making progress. He has actually stopped feeding Cement at the table, which Mum says she is very grateful to Karl for. Unfortunately, Cement does eat any old thing he finds on the floor, which is still a very bad habit. Karl says they will work on this behaviour.

Mum says she can't wait.

Karl says, 'If I don't do my dog walking, then I won't save enough money to buy my Christmas presents and I will be letting everyone down, *including* my dog customers.'

I know how he feels.

I say, 'I don't know how I'm going to have enough money to buy all the ingredients for my fudge.'

Karl says,

'I don't like fudge.'

Then he just carries on talking like this is a normal thing to say, even though I have never, ever met anyone who has ever said this before.

Because who doesn't like fudge?

I am so in SHOCK about this that I can't concentrate on anything he is saying so I mainly just walk along and nod, but his words aren't going into my ears. All I can think about now is this new problem on my plate.

What am I going to get Karl?

And *how*? when I have no extra money left in the toadstool and I still need £3.20 plus a stamp

if I'm going to have enough to purchase the
RUBY FLY LIGHT?

Imagine NOT liking fudge.

At the top of our street I have to walk past Mrs
Stampney and she DOESN'T say, 'By the way,
thank you, Clarice Bean, for the handmade
Christmas card. How kind of you to think of me
even though I am very mean and crabby.' What
she DOES say is, 'Could you tell that brother of
yours to turn his music down? It's very LOUD
and it's coming through the walls.'

So I say, 'Actually it's my sister, Marcie,
     who's the one playing the loud music.'

Mrs Stampney says, 'Well, you can tell her from
me that the music she listens to is most unladylike!'
And I say, 'I will definitely tell her. I know
Marcie will be very pleased to hear that.

     Merry Christmas, Mrs Stampney!'

And then I run along on as quick as I can,
all the way home.

When I get in Mum asks me how the last day
of school went.

     I say, 'Good.'

She says, 'So how did it go with your Christmas cards?'

I say, 'Good.'

She says, 'Did it make Grace and Cindy happy that you made one for them too?' and I say, 'You know what, it actually really DID,' and she says, 'I told you so.'

And I say, 'It didn't work on Mrs Stampney,' and Mum says, 'NOTHING does.'

Mum is busy making some angel cakes. She says she has to bake at least seventy, which is a lot. They are for the party at the old people's centre. She says, 'I have a horrible feeling I miscalculated the quantities and they may well turn out to be soufflés or, even worse, biscuits.'

I say, 'I think biscuits are nicer than cakes,' and she says, 'Thank you.'

I say, 'Don't worry, I bet everyone will eat them anyway, whatever they taste like.'

She says, 'To be honest, I am past caring. I'm just looking forward to sitting down on a sofa covered in crumbs with my feet up.'

And this makes me feel bad because crumbs can

be quite uncomfortable, especially if you are wearing tights. So I get hoovering.

And Mum calls out, 'Clarice Bean, I can't tell you what music it is to hear the drone of a vacuum cleaner.'

And when she sits down, she says, 'What a joy to sit in comfort. Thank you!'

And I say, 'It's no big deal.'

Which is what Ruby Redfort would say.

And Mum says, 'Sometimes it's the SMALL things that make the BIGGEST difference.'

Which is true because it turns out to have the benefit of three pounds seventy-six pence in SMALL change lost under the cushions. If I'm allowed to keep it as mine then I have enough to send off for the special offer RUBY FLY LIGHT and still have exactly approximately the right amount for the fudge ingredients.

Mum says, 'As far as I'm concerned, if you vacuum the sofa, it's finders keepers.'

Because there is not a moment to lose I quickly put on my shoes and nip to the post office. Luckily, I have already filled out the coupon with my name and address, so I just hand over the money and the post office turn it into a postal order and pop it into the envelope and send it off.

Now all I have to do is cross my fingers that the **FLY LIGHT** will arrive before Betty goes.

After supper me and Grandad watch a programme about wolves and how ALL dogs started off as wolves and that who could believe a Chihuahua was once a wolf?

And thinking about this reminds me of Frank who is a Chihuahua Karl walks, and then we start talking about Karl.

I say, 'He is very in the dumps.'

Grandad says, 'And why's that then?'

And then we talk about Alf's cold and Karl needing to stay home to keep him company while Jean-next-door is always on the phone.

I say, 'Alf doesn't like being by himself with Jean-next-door because she forgets to talk to him but if Karl stays home too then Karl can't do his dog walking and can't save up his Christmas money.'

Grandad says, 'What a pickle.'

And I tell Grandad how I am in the same boat for different reasons and have no money for Karl's present because he doesn't like fudge.

Grandad says, 'Who doesn't like fudge?'

I say, 'I know!'

Grandad says, 'One thing that's worth thinking about is that a Christmas present doesn't have to be an actual thing – it can be a kindness or a helpful hand.'

And then he says, 'Sometimes it's the SMALLEST

things that make the BIGGEST difference.'
And this is interesting because it's exactly
what Mum said.

Just before bed when I am brushing my teeth
Marcie comes into the bathroom. I step slightly
away from the sink so she can catch sight of
my Christmas list. I expect her to show some
interest but all she says is, 'You'll be lucky.'
She doesn't mean, 'I'm sure your wish will come
true.' She actually means, 'For your information,
there is no chance of you getting any of this.'
If I hadn't read **RUBY REDFORT**, then I might
agree with her point of view, but I have, so I know
she is wrong.

So I say the same thing Ruby Redfort would say:

'How can your wishes come TRUE,
if you NEVER even
bother to wish?'

FIVE

Joy to the World

IN THE MORNING I AM WOKEN LOUDLY by Marcie calling up the stairs. She has a very piercing voice and it comes right into my dream. She says, **'Peggy's on the phone for YOU.'** And I am very surprised because Peggy has never phoned for me before.

I *rush down* with bleary eyes. She says, 'Clarice Bean, I've had a thought about your singing. Do you have a spare minute?' And I say, 'Yes,' and she says, 'Then pop your warmest coat on and come right over,' and I run to Peggy's as quickly as I can. There is a shopping trolley parked in front of her gate and I have to twizzle it away before I can ring the doorbell.

When Peggy answers I say,

'Peggy, did you know there is a
shopping trolley lurking by your house?'
And she says, 'Oh, not AGAIN!

There's someone who keeps leaving
trolleys in the street and it is driving me
COMPLETELY round the bend.'
We talk about this for a few minutes or so
and then Peggy says,

'Let's not waste our time with
abandoned shopping trolleys when there are
better things to think about.
How FAR can you count
on ONE BREATH?'
And I say,

'1 2 3 4 5 6 7 8 9 10 11 12 13 14 15 16 17 18 19 20 21 22,'

and she says,

'Not bad, but now let's do that again
without letting the numbers
run away from you.'

We keep doing this over and over. I take a deep breath IN and I slowly breathe OUT the numbers until I have not the TINIEST bit of air left in me. Peggy says, 'If you keep practising this exercise, you will find you can manage more numbers and they will sound less wobbly because you

will be more IN CONTROL of your breath which means the notes you sing will be

STEADIER and more tuneful.'

Then she says, 'Take another breath – hold it, are you holding it?'

I just nod because I am, which means I can't speak.

'Imagine you are a balloon and the air is

very s l o w l y hissing out through a GAP in your teeth. Make it last as L O N G as you can.'

'H i S s S s S s S s s s S s s...'

I find I am very good at this. I think it's because I acted as a snake in the school play once. Hiss was the ONLY line I had.

Next, Peggy teaches me how to breathe right down into my actual toes.

You can tell if you're doing this right if you lie

on the carpet with your hands on your tummy. What should happen is when you breathe IN, your tummy fills up with air so it is sticking OUT, and then your chest fills up with air and you won't believe how much air you can get into your body if you use your stomach too. When you breathe OUT, you go completely FLAT. After learning the breathing, Peggy teaches me how to warm up for singing, which is deep breaths with a yawn at the end because yawning opens up your throat.

I say, 'It's a very strange thing to do, Peggy.' And she says, 'You might NOT believe it, Clarice, but I have a singing friend, called Tiu de Haan, who warms up her voice by mooing.'

I say, 'Like a COW?'

She says, 'Exactly. Tiu says she has mooed in all the most famous concert halls in the world.'

I say, 'Which should I do, mooing or yawning?'

Peggy says, 'Moo when you are practising making a BIG sound, yawn when you want to practise taking a BIG breath. Just don't mind what anybody else thinks – that's the trick.'

'Now,' she says,

'STAND
like
a
superhero,

very STRONG

and STRAIGHT,

imagining your cape f l o w i n g
out behind you. Are you ready?'

'Ready,' I say.

'So NOW we will sing!'

And we do.

When we have finished all our exercises Peggy
says, 'You know, your Mrs Wilberton is quite
WRONG about your voice. You sing like an
angel, Clarice Bean, and I will be sure to tell
her so when I see her.'
So of course I skip home in an utterly good mood.
Peggy is one of those people who always
makes you feel good.
Grandad says this is a RARE talent.
I can see why Peggy is his best friend.

The phone is r¹ng¹ng and r¹ng¹ng when I get in.
No one is answering it and I *rush* to pick it up
before it gets bored and STOPS.
I say, 'This is Clarice Bean speaking,'
and the phone says,
'This is Granny speaking,' back.
Me: 'Oh, hello, Granny.'
Granny: 'Did you get a parcel?'
Me: 'Yes.'
Granny: 'From America?'
Me: 'No.'
Granny: 'Bother!'
Me: 'Why?'

Granny: 'It should have reached you by now.'

Me: 'Oh.'

Granny: 'I think it's going to arrive very late.'

Me: 'How do you know?'

Granny: 'My friend Wallace says there's some problem at the shipping depot and that if they haven't managed to launch your parcel by now then it won't arrive until after Christmas.'

Me: 'Oh.'

Granny: 'I know.'

Me: 'Don't worry, Granny. It will be something to look forward to.'

Granny: 'Well, that's very kind of you to say, Clarice, because I am feeling dreadful about letting you all down like this.'

Me: 'It's not your fault.'

I am feeling dreadful too because I can see our parcel for Granny NOT posted. It's sitting there underneath Mr Felixstow's Christmas appeal parcel on the stool next to the fridge. Inside the package are all our Christmas presents to her in New York including the TINY-USEFUL-THINGS BAG and if no one puts it in the letterbox it will mean she has nothing to open from us. And we don't even have the true excuse of the problem at the depot.

Our excuse is we can't be bothered to walk to the post office.

Granny and I talk about what's going on in her apartment block. Which is mainly that there is a loose rodent somewhere in the walls but no one is sure what it is up to and whether it is alone.

Granny says, 'How they get IN is what beats me.'

I say, 'Luckily we DON'T have this problem of wall rodents.'

Granny says, 'They can probably

smell Cement and this puts them off.'
I say, 'It would certainly put me off
if I was a rat with choices.'
Cement has got into the habit of rolling in
unpleasant things my dad says might be to do
with foxes, so he is not smelling very pleasing,
and Granny says, 'I imagine not.'
Once we have covered all the important things
like:

What I'm reading: **RUBY REDFORT**,
  CATCH YOUR DEATH

What she's reading: **How to Rid Your Home
  of Unwanted Pests and Rodents**

What I am going to be WATCHING later
What she's going to be WATCHING later
What we are having for TEA
What she's having for LUNCH

we say goodbye, which takes a few goes because
we always remember one last thing we forgot to
remember, and of course I say, 'We will call you
on Christmas Day.'
And she says, 'I will be waiting by the telephone.'

It is only when I put the phone down that I realise that I have accidentally been nibbling the edges off the lemon drizzle cake. It might not matter except there is a note next to it that says:

Clarice Bean
Please do NOT nibble the edges
of the LEMON DRIZZLE cake.

I hope no one notices.

Then I tip out the emergency money from the just-in-case tin, find the pre-addressed labels, grab Granny's Christmas parcel and Mr Felixstow's Christmas parcel, put them in Grandad's drag-along shopping trolley and *run like the wind* to the post office. Luckily the wind is going my way. I stick the labels on the packages. Mr Felixstow's parcel isn't too bad but Granny's weighs a fortune and I only just have enough money to cover the AIRMAIL stamps and have a bit left over for a Yogga-Pop.

On my way out of the post office I bump into
Marguerite – who is my aunt but we just call her
Marguerite. She is pushing her bike with the cart
thing on the front that my cousin Yolla sometimes
sits in. Today it is not filled with Yolla but with
lots of stacked-up food in dishes and pots.
Marguerite looks utterly weighed down with
shopping bags and has given up cycling.
She's just trudging along.
She says, 'I can't cycle against this wind.'
I say, 'Where are you going?' and she tells me
she is delivering to the old-people's centre
because it is their Christmas party today
and, since she has a day off from work,
she is helping out.
I say, 'I can put some of the things in my
                    trolley if you like?'
And she says, 'I can't say I couldn't use the help.'
So that's what we do and she looks relieved.
She says, 'It's such a shame
        we WON'T be seeing you at Christmas.
We are going to miss you all so much.'
I say, 'Why don't you come?'

She says, 'Well, if only
we hadn't made our
Christmas plans
back in January,
we would have
invited you ALL
to ours.'

OFFICE

72

I say, 'Do you **always** make your Christmas plans in January?'

And she says, 'Not normally, but our friends the Robertses asked us five days after Christmas when we were feeling like we'd really had enough of it all and the idea of being somewhere else with other people doing all the cooking sounded lovely.'

Marguerite doesn't look like someone who is thinking this is a lovely idea.

She says, 'The thing is, Clarice Bean, and I know I shouldn't say this . . .'

Marguerite always says *I know I shouldn't say this* when she is about to tell you something you are not normally told by a grown-up.

So I wait and she says, '. . . but I sort of wish we weren't going.'

I say, 'What about Al?'

Al is my uncle but we always just call him Al.

And she says, 'He wishes we weren't going.'

I say, 'Me too.'

She says, 'I wish we were coming to *you*.'

I say, 'Me too.'

She says, 'The Robertses are fun, but . . .'

I say, 'I know.' Although I don't know because

I have never even heard of the Robertseses.

And she says, '. . . and actually I love doing all
the cooking,'
and I say, 'I know.'

'And it's so far to drive . . . and we will have to set
off on Christmas Eve . . . early . . . very early.'

I say, 'Oh,' because I don't know what to say.
But it doesn't matter because I think she is talking
to herself more than me.

She says, 'I love Christmas Eve but we'll be
in the car for most of it . . . and Noah gets so
car sick . . . we will be stopping and starting.'

I am listening to her and you can see she feels like
she is already in the car and it does not look like
a nice place to be.

I say, 'Maybe something good will happen and
the Robertseses will get terrible tummy bugs
and ask you not to come because they don't
feel like cooking!'

Marguerite seems very cheered up by this thought.
She is smiling a LOT – she almost looks like she
might laugh.

Then she says, 'Talking of cooking, you should

see what I have made for the centre – I hope they
will like it.'

I say, 'Well, I know they will be really pleased,
because you are an exceptionOrdinarily
good cook.'

And she says, 'Well, thank you, Clarice Bean.
You have cheered me up no end.'

When we arrive at the centre
Mum says, 'Fancy seeing you
here, Clarice Bean.'

And Marguerite says,
    'She has been
        such a help.'

Once I have unloaded the
trolley and all the other
things, I decide to stay
on at the centre and
help Marguerite set up
the table and heat the
dishes and serve all
the food out with
her and Mum
and Reg.

Marguerite says, 'It's lucky I ran into you,
        Clarice Bean. You have made my day.'
And I feel the same because all my good deeds are
bringing back the Christmas spirit.
Mum says she is very glad to have an extra pair of
hands because it is hard to serve lunch and talk
to all the residents and make sure everyone is
having a good time.

I like the
        chatting.

I chat to Mr Flanders, mainly about biscuits
        but then we both wonder if there is
        going to be life on Mars.

I also chat to Brenda who has
        a tricky ingrowing toenail.

I know lots of the residents and they tend to
tell me interesting things like this.

★ ★ ★

Once we've cleared up we walk home together
very pleased with myself.
I tell her about the posting the parcels off.
And Mum says, 'Goodness, Clarice Bean, you
have been spreading the Christmas spirit today!'
And when Dad gets back she tells him about this
too, and about helping Marguerite, and serving
lunch at the centre.
And it is a perfect Christmas moment like one
of those cards where the families are smiling
at each other in front of the fireplace, except
Minal points at me and says,
'Clarice has been nibbling the edges off the
lemon drizzle cake when you aren't looking.'
So I have to pinch him on the leg of course,
which takes me down a notch,
              which is NOT MY FAULT.
Mum looks inside the emergency tin for cash
so she can send Kurt down to the shop for fish
fingers. She says,
    'Where's all the just-in-case money?'

I say I spent it on the stamps for the parcels to Granny and Mr Felix-whatsit.

And she says, 'Was there not any change left over?'

I say, 'No, it came to quite a lot in the end and there was only enough left over for one Yogga-Pop.'

And she says, 'Goodness that was expensive – I know the parcel to Mr Felixstow was very heavy but even so . . .'

I say, 'It was Granny's parcel that was the expensive one.'

And Mum says, 'But that one was so light. Airmail must have got a lot more pricey lately.'

I am beginning to get a slight worry that something might have gone wrong with the labelling. So I decide the best idea is not to think about it.

Kurt goes off to buy the fish fingers and everyone is in a good mood and there are crisps before dinner. Dinner is very nice and everyone is allowed as much tomato ketchup as they want.

Afterwards we all squash on to the sofa to watch the second part of the **RUBY REDFORT CHRISTMAS SPECIAL** but the suspense is interrupted by Cement who is barking at the not-blown-out Advent candle, which is still flickering on the table.

Grandad says, 'I think he gets very stressed by flames.'

Mum says, 'Yes, I think it's ever since the wok caught fire.'

I jump up and *run* into the kitchen to *blow* it out but Minal gets there first. And then we get into an argument. Which ends up with us grabbing sleeves and *slipping* on the floor.

By the time I have given Minal an arm twist and he has given me a bruise on the leg, I have completely MISSED nearly the whole last four minutes of the **RUBY CHRISTMAS SPECIAL**.

I race back just in time to hear Ruby say,

'Tell it to the elves,
SUCKER!'

I have no idea who the 'SUCKER' is

but I think it

might

be

me.

SIX

Merrily on High

AT BREAKFAST IT IS JUST ME AND GRANDAD
listening to the Christmas radio songs, eating our
Sugar Puffs. I'm not sure where everyone else has
gone but it is very quiet except for the tree branch
outside, which keeps tapping at the window.
Grandad says he's had an idea.
He says,
  'I asked Peggy about it and she said
    she thought it was a good one.'
And I wait for him to tell me what the idea is.
Grandad says, 'I ALWAYS trust Peggy.
    She always knows what's right,'
and then he starts talking about something else
Peggy once said when he lost his keys in the park.

t is quite a long story, which is rambling on
and making me fidget.
So I say, 'Grandad, WHAT is your idea that
            Peggy agrees is a good one?'
He says,

            'Help walk the dogs.'
I am not sure what he is talking about but then
Mum comes out of the larder and says,
        'He means Karl's dogs
                and Karl's mother's dogs –
        if *you* help walk them,
then Karl can earn his Christmas money
and Mrs Wrenbury can stay home
        with Karl's brother and this can be
                your Christmas present to Karl.'

I say, 'But two of us isn't enough,'
and Grandad says,
            'But me and Peggy will help
and together we would be able to manage
        his two dog customers as well as
                his mother's five dog customers
                            and Cement.'

It is a very remarkable idea and I agree with it.
So Grandad calls Karl's mum and she says,
'Yes, that will really cheer him up.'
Then she says, 'And, you know what,
        I would love to stay home with Alf
                and watch the Muppets.'

And so me and Grandad and Cement walk over
the hill to the block of flats where Karl lives.
We can see Karl and his mum waving to us from
the second-floor balcony. Alf is waving next to her
in a bobble hat and a far-too-big coat.
Karl's mum calls down,
        'Karl knows where to pick up
                the dogs so he will lead the way.'
Grandad calls back, 'Righto.'
Karl's mum calls out,
'I can't tell you what this means to Karl.'
Karl makes a stupid face at his mum and Karl's
mum pulls his hat down over his eyes.
And she calls out,
        'Thanks so much!'
and Alf calls out, 'Thanks so much.'

Then she shouts,

   'Now we are going to watch the Muppets,'

      and Alf shouts,

         'Now we are going to
             watch the Muppets,'

and they turn to go back indoors

      and Alf shouts,
'And we're going to make some paper chains,'

         and Karl's mum shouts,
            'And make paper chains.'

We collect all the various seven dogs from their houses and then we go off to find Peggy.

She is
sitting on
a bench
by
the park gate.

She says, 'I'm wearing my good vest.'

I say, 'So am I.'

Peggy says, 'That's good.

A singer must take care of their lungs –
keep the chest warm.'

It's not actually that cold but it is very *blowy*
on the hill and it is hard to walk seven dogs
plus Cement all at the same time.

The SMALLEST one, which is a Chihuahua called
Frank, is finding it very difficult to walk
because he is being *blown* to a STOP and is
mainly stationary so in the end Peggy puts
him in her shopping bag

and Frank looks relieved.

Karl says this is not a good thing to do on
a regular basis but in an emergency it is OK.

It is a very nice day even with the wind and there
are lots of people and lots of dogs out today.

Several of the dogs we meet on the hill are
wearing Christmas coats and collars.

One is a pug in antlers.

Karl does not really approve of antlers on a dog.

He says, 'Dogs are not toys.'

I agree but secretly think if I had a pug I would
put antlers on it.
Betty always dresses up her dog, Ralph,
who is a Pekinese and Ralph doesn't mind a bit –
this year he will be a choirboy.
We won't tell Karl.
Peggy has brought her Thermos flask so we can all
have a hot drink on a bench.
She asks Karl if he has done his Christmas
shopping yet, and he says he's hoping to do it
after the dog-walking.
He wants to look in the shops to see if he can find
some presents for his mum and his brother, Alf.
He says, 'I also want to get one for
Mrs Tomassini – she makes dinner for me
    and Alf on Tuesday and Wednesday when my
mum has to work. She makes really nice things
        and she's teaching me to cook too.'
Peggy says, 'It's a wonderful thing to know
how to cook.'
He says, 'I can do macaroni cheese now.
It's not a normal one – it's got all sorts in it.'
I say, 'It sounds quite advanced.'

And he says,
      'It's not as tricky as all that –
I'm sure you'd be able to do it.
            You just have to know how.'
And Peggy says,
      'So what are you thinking of getting
         Mrs Tomassini for Christmas?'
Karl says,
   'Well, I was thinking about
      a wooden spoon, you know,
         for stirring? But do you think
      she might already have one?'
Peggy says,
   'You can never have
too many wooden spoons
   if you like cooking.'
She says,
   'Sometimes you can find
those ones you can
         hang up by a string.'

Karl likes this idea.

There is something about
the wind when it is warm
like this that makes you feel
like you want to RUN.
And we do, we ALL run

round and round and round.

The dogs look VERY happy too.
Karl says,
'It's easy to tell when a dog is happy –
it's all in their tails.'
But I think you can also know from their faces.
To me it is obvious they are smiling,
and Peggy agrees.

After our walk, we drop off the dogs and Grandad
gives Karl an envelope with *Happy Christmas*
written on it and says, 'Just a little something
to say thank you for helping me
train Cement.'

Grandad and Peggy go to the Polish café next to
Eggplant for another cup of tea. Me and Karl
wander along Park Road and he nips into shops
while I stand outside with Cement, and then I
nip into the corner shop to buy my ingredients
while Karl and Cement wait outside.
The last shop is the cookery shop and Karl is in
there ages trying to choose a spoon.
I say, 'What took you so long?'
and Karl shows me the spoon and says,
'I wanted one that you can hang up by a string,
but they didn't have any.'
I say, 'It's still very nice.'
Karl says, 'Do you think she will like it?'
and I say, 'I would,' which is actually true
even though I don't need a wooden spoon.
I invite Karl back to ours for tea and Karl
shows Mum the spoon and he says,
'Maybe it's a bit boring.'
And she says, 'Not at all,
but if you wanted to we could
drill a SMALL hole in the end
of the handle.

I've got some stripy
string you could
thread through and
then Mrs Tomassini
could hang it up.'
And Karl says, 'That's exactly
what I was wanting!'
They work on it together
and he goes home really happy.
He shouts, 'Thank you for the spoon help,
Mrs Tuesday, and thank you for the
dog-walking, Clarice Bean! It was a really
good Christmas present!'
It is so windy outside that his voice is almost
blown away but I'm sure I can just hear
him say, 'I've got a really good idea for your
Christmas present, Clarice . . .

Just wait and see!'

SEVEN

Christmas Tree Oh Christmas Tree

TODAY IS MY SECOND-MOST FAVOURITE day before Christmas because it's the day we get our tree. We tend to get our tree a long time after everyone else in our street because Mum says if you get them too early they drop needles all over the carpet. Mum usually comes with us because she knows how big a tree is allowed to be before it won't fit in the room, but she can't come today because she is working at the old-people's centre again due to short-staffing.
As she is leaving the house, she calls out,

'Remember, not too BIG!'

Dad and me and Minal go down to the Christmas-tree place, which is basically a HUGE yard with nothing but trees propped round.
Grandad is banned from coming on these trips because he always picks the sad trees.
They are called the sad trees because Mum says they look like they are crying pine needles, i.e. they are already a bit dried up and on their last legs.
Most of them are all leaning about, tied up with string, and so it's hard to know what they will turn out like once they are freed.
So we look at the ones that are on display.
There are so many to choose from I can't make up my mind.

I wander around the trees,
up and down the rows of them,
and I try NOT to touch any of them because
I don't want to give them hope that they are
the chosen one.
It is really hard to make the right choice because
they are different shapes from each other,
and some have nice gaps between the branches,
and some have nice needles.
There are so many different breeds.
Although Dad says when you are talking about
trees you are meant to say species.
He says, 'Breeds is for dogs.'
So I say, 'Dad, how would you choose
a species of tree?'
And he says, 'Just pick the one you think will
fit in the car.'
This of course is NOT a good way to pick a
perfect tree but luckily Dad bumps into
someone he knows from work called Mr Oberon,
so I know we are going to be here for ages,
which means there is plenty of time
to find the right one.

Since I would prefer to look in peace,
I decide it might be BEST
if I lose Minal.

I do this by hiding
for a minute in a clump
of perched-together
Christmas trees and I can hear Minal Cricket

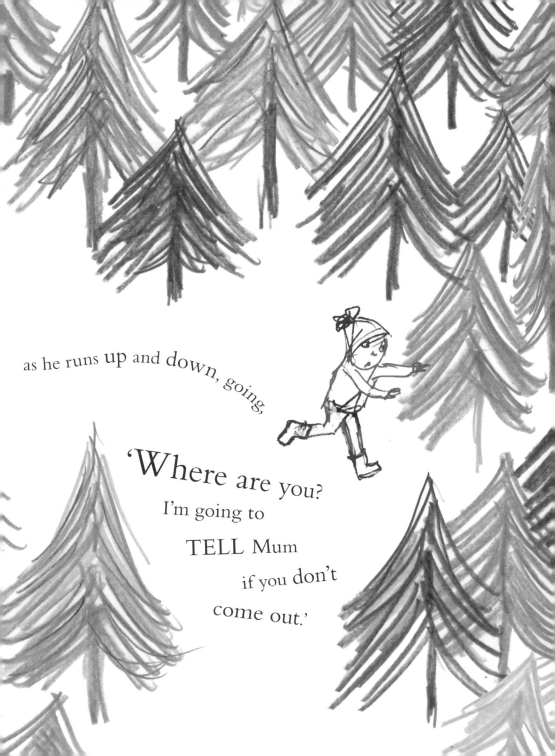

as he runs up and down, going,

'Where are you?
I'm going to
TELL Mum
if you don't
come out.'

It's important to keep your breathing to a minimum and NOT sneeze if you want to keep out of your enemy's clutches. It's also a good idea to avoid chewing bubble gum. Ruby Redfort could tell you a lot about this since she got captured once by several arch villains in the book **CATCH YOUR DEATH** and it was due to the smell of Hubble Yum bubble gum. Thinking about Ruby Redfort makes me want to read my book, which, luckily, I have with me. I get so caught up in the plot, which is actually set in a forest that I completely forget to look for trees.

★ ★ ★

When Dad finally finishes chatting, I reappear like magic and he says, 'So which tree is it to be?' And Minal says, 'This one,' and points to a tree that is twelve feet high.
Dad says, 'This is not going to fit in our living room, let alone the car.'
Minal starts whining. 'But it's the best one!'
Dad says, 'Jeepers, Minal, we can't even carry it.'

So of course my brother tries to pick it up,
which is not possible for someone who is a squirt.
  It topples on top of him
          and he is trapped underneath it.
Minal is making this weird sound and at first we
think he is injured and in requirement of a medical
assistant but then we realise it is the sound of
trapped giggling.
Minal Cricket has a strange giggle which sounds
more like a piglet than a boy. It is one of those
catching types of laughs and Dad finds it very easy
to contract laughing so he is set off by Minal.
This makes the tree-selling man quite cross
because all he can see from where he is, is a man
who is more than forty laughing at a fallen-over
Christmas tree.
I shout, 'Don't worry! He is NOT laughing at
    the tree – he's laughing because there is a
          SMALL boy trapped under it.'
This does not sound at all funny to the man and
he starts getting agitated about safety and health
and so Dad has to extract Minal on the double
before we get reported to the child protectors.

Dad says, 'Look, he's fine!'
When the tree-selling man sees that Minal is not
injured he gets very cross indeed and Dad
goes a bit pale-ish when he is informed that
due to damage to several branches,
we are going to have to buy this tree
whether we like it or not.

The laughing is ended.

Dad goes into a decline and says he is going in
search of a cup of coffee because the idea of
getting a twelve-foot tree into a
less-than-twelve-foot car is sending his
energy levels in a downwards direction.

In the end we have to call Uncle Ted and ask him
for his assistance. Uncle Ted is a firefighter so of
course he is used to dealing with emergencies and
getting a tree into a car should not be a problem.
He has brought a saw with him and he chops

off some of the trunk and we sort of manage
to WEDGE it so it's mostly in the car but not
quite all. Uncle Ted ties Minal's jumper to the
sticking-out-of-the-car bit as a warning that we
are dangerous. Minal is NOT pleased and starts
gribbling, but Dad explains that it is all his
own fault, so i.e. put a sock in it.
On the drive back I find myself sitting in the
branches and I have an idea of what it might
be like to be a squirrel.

When we get home there is a realisation that the
tree is very big and more than was expected in as
far as how much it sticks out.
We have to move most of the furniture to the
edges. When Mum gets home from work she has
to walk *sideways* into the room.
Everyone is waiting for her to say something with
her arms folded and a lemon-lip look but when
she sees Dad's face, which seems a bit down in
the eyes, she just says,
   'I think it's nice to bring the outside in.'
And everyone looks relieved and has a cup of tea.

But the **problem** is that we have got a **very large** tree in our house which is **not allowing** us to sit comfortably in **chairs**

and it's hard to
see round the
branches.

Minal and me have started another argument
about the tree, which is not my fault.
I only pointed out that he is to blame and
should be in trouble. Marcie has joined in by
telling us we are both annoying so we tell her
that this is none of her beeswax and Kurt tells
us to shut up because we are ALL boring.

So now everyone starts SHOUTING.

Mum says,
        'Do you think we should put it outside?
It could look nice in the garden?'
Uncle Ted says, 'It might be a good idea
because this tree is going to make it impossible
for you to ALL be in the same room together.'
Dad says,
        'In that case let's keep it where it is.'
But then Grandad wakes up from his armchair and
panics because he thinks he is lost in a forest.
It takes him a few minutes to feel sure that he
is indoors.
Even so he decides to put his coat on.

He says, 'I'll have my tea out of the Thermos flask.'
Mum says, 'Why?'
and he says, 'Because I always do when
I'm outside.'
Mum says, 'You are in the sitting room.'
He says, 'I know you *say* that, but it doesn't
feel like it.'
Mum goes to get the clippers and does some
pruning, which means we can move the furniture
back to mainly where it's supposed to be.
Then she winds the lights round from the top to
the bottom, only they run out in the middle and
she says, 'I'm going to need at least two more
strings of them.'
Uncle Ted offers to go and buy some more but it
is decided that he cannot be trusted to choose the
right kind of tree lights so Marcie is sent out
grumbling.
Once that's sorted Mum has to get on with
the supper, so I put all the decorations and
thingummyjigs on the branches. The technique
is to make sure that everything ISN'T all
clumped together.

My favourites are the glass ones in different shapes, which are treasured heirlooms of the family. Some are elves and some are angels, and most of them are very old and from before I was born. I also like the felt ones, which are horses, and the wooden ones, which are toadstools.

I don't know why toadstools are for Christmas, but they look good.

Mum says, 'You have to spread them all evenly and don't just put all the nice ones on one side and the not-so-nice ones round the back.'

I say, 'Why do we bother having the not-so-nice decorations?'

and Mum says, 'Because we are sentimental about them.'

I'm not sure why she is sentimental about Minal's decorations – they are just macaroni and there is plenty of that in the larder.

I get decorating and I am doing well with the spreading them out until something interesting comes on the television and it is only when it's finished that I realise all the decorations are facing the telly.

I am standing on a stepladder, trying to move some toadstools and elves to the other side of the tree when I am almost

toppled off
by Minal, who starts jumping
up and down,
squeaking.
And I have to
GRAB on to the tree
to hold my balance,
and
I let go of several
elves and they
S M A S H
on the floor
and Mum rushes to rescue the tree from
falling completely over on top of me
and she bumps into Grandad's cup of tea which
luckily is cold because it goes all over Grandad's
trouser legs and Mum loses her temper.

She says,

   'Minal, *SHRIEKING*
      and jumping UP and DOWN
   is ABSOLUTELY banned!
Just LOOK what
     you've done!'

And he says, 'But I saw the fox,
      like the one in my book.'
And Mum says, 'Your fox book is banned!'
And Minal says, 'But—'
And Mum puts her finger up, which means
      'No buts!'
and Minal is in the dog house because he has
destroyed the ancient Christmas decorations.
There are no elves left and they all have to
be hoovered up into the vacuum cleaner and
Grandad's trousers have to go in to soak.
Mum looks sad about the elves. She says,
'They belonged to my grandmother,'
and I say, 'And now they are gone forever.'
And Mum sighs in a deep way and says, 'Oh well,
they gave us great joy while they lasted.'

But I didn't want them to stop lasting
and I wish they could be put back together
because I'm not sure we can do without elves.
Because, you see,

everyone

needs

elves

at

Christmas.

EIGHT

Deck the Halls with Boughs of Holly

IT IS THE DAY BEFORE CHRISTMAS EVE
and it is the day of the school carol concert.
All the shopping has been done – except for Dad's.
He hasn't started his yet but that's normal and
Mum doesn't even bother to be surprised.
Mum and Dad have to go out somewhere and they
have asked me to be in charge of answering the
door to the turkey person because Kurt will have
his headphones on and Mum says, 'There is not
a chance he will hear the doorbell ping.'
She says, 'When it arrives shout up to your
brother and get him to take it down the garden
where there is now a fridge in the shed.'

She says, 'You will need help because your father accidentally ordered the massively LARGE one.' Dad says, 'Whatever you do, do not try to squeeze the turkey into the fridge in the kitchen or it will be chaos.'

They have also asked me to be in charge of making a cup of tea and a slice of lemon drizzle for Mrs Rippon who has 'kindly offered to come in at a moment's notice to do a one-off clean and polish of all the floors'. Dad says the floors are so dirty that they are a danger to germs.

Mum says, 'I've baked a fresh lemon drizzle cake so please *do not nibble it!*'

Mum says she feels she can trust me to do all this because it seems at last some of Betty Moody's responsible influence has rubbed off on me.

She doesn't have much choice because Marcie and Grandad and Minal are going to be in and out for most of the day, coming and going, and Mum says she has lost track of who's home when so it's all down to me.

She says, 'Mrs Rippon will let herself in with her key.'

Then mostly everyone goes off and the house is quiet. I want to prove that I am to be trusted because it gets you extra points with Father Christmas and you need a lot of points to get a piano, so I decide to wait on a stool by the door. This way I won't miss the turkey's arrival. I've got my **RUBY REDFORT** word-searcher puzzle book so it's not as boring as you might think.

By the time the doorbell goes I am very desperate for the toilet. I have to *run* for it as soon as I've wished *a very merry Christmas* to the turkey person who is a woman, who turns out to be a very keen chatter and has a badge, which is holly that flickers.

I shout up to Kurt, but Mum and Dad are right and he does NOT hear a blimming thing and I can't be bothered to go and yell through his bedroom door because he will only grumble. The turkey is very hard to move so I have to take it out of its box and carry it like a heavy baby wrapped in paper.

I think about taking it down the garden in the wheelbarrow, but it is raining so instead

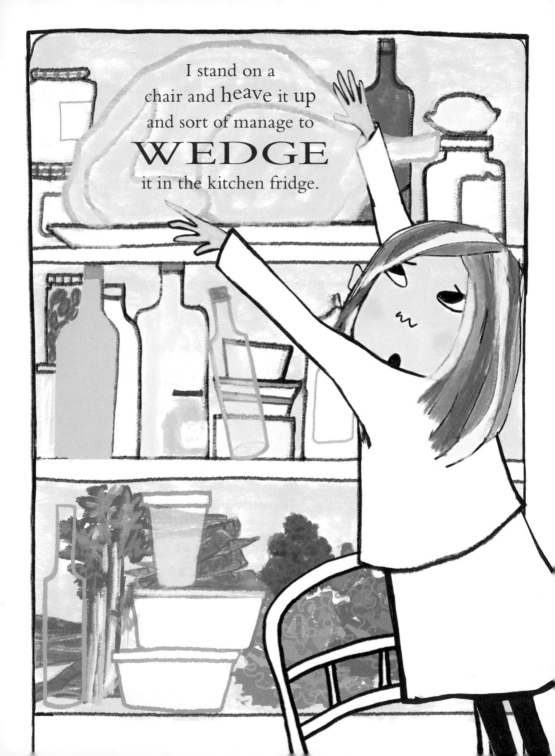

I am pleased because there is no chaos at all
and so now I can think about having a little relax
before Mrs Rippon takes over the kitchen.
Of course, that's when I realise that the lemon
drizzle is now stuck BEHIND the turkey.
Mum put it in the fridge to hide it from nibblers.
I have to cautiously open the door and feel
around with my hand. It is WEDGED in the
back and I can only get to it by manoeuvring the
turkey outwards and dropping it on the floor.
I am wondering how I am going to get the energy
to pick it up when the doorbell goes. Since I am
expecting no one else to answer it, I have to.
And there is the postman with a large elastic band
of letters. I am hopeful that the RUBY FLY LIGHT
will be one of them but it is NOT there.
They are ALL but one addressed to the Tuesday
family which is us, so I am allowed by law
to open them. It takes quite a while and by the
time I have arranged the cards all over the place
I realise I have completely forgotten I was meant
to be lifting a turkey off the floor.

I nip back to the kitchen but strangely the **turkey** is NOT where I left it and has moved itself to the **back door**. It doesn't look quite the **same shape** as it did before – something oddish has happened and it has a nibbled look. I think it has definitely been chewed by possibly a dog and is NOT fit for human consumption, especially because the kitchen floor is still a hygiene hazard.

I instantly

have

a **bad** feeling

and am

FROZEN

with panic.

Ruby Redfort says: PANIC will freeze your brain and of course she is right, and I sit at the table for a few minutes STARING at the lemon drizzle, wondering what to do.

Ruby often says that when you fear for your life it is a good idea to go to your nearest safe space. So I shut myself in the downstairs toilet.

It is not actually my actual safe space but it has a lock and a toilet.

I am thinking Dad was right about not putting a too-big turkey in a full-up fridge and how it is now chaos.

While I am locked in I hear quite a lot of different-sized footsteps plus slippers passing by, which is actually the sound of Mrs Rippon.

Minal is gabbling on at her about foxes and so I decide to stay put until I can make a clean getaway.

I only manage to distract myself from possible doom by doing fifteen or so word searches. One of the words in the search is CAKE, and this reminds me how I would love a slice of lemon drizzle. I want it so much I can almost taste it, which is when I realise that actually I *can* taste it because I must have accidentally nibbled the corners while panic was FREEZING my brain. I am already in enough trouble due to the chewed turkey without Mum finding out about the cake-nibbling.

So as soon as I hear Mrs Rippon leave without a cup of tea, I unlock the door and tiptoe into the kitchen.

No one is there and so I slice the nibbled bit of cake and quickly eat it before anyone can know. This is called EATING THE EVIDENCE and is what Ruby Redfort would advise me to do in this situation.

Mum will think Mrs Rippon has eaten it and will never know that it was me.

Then I nip upstairs to the airing cupboard. While I am waiting in there, I am thinking about my unfortunate situation and what I can do to wriggle out of it.

I am tempted to add a TURKEY to my Father Christmas list but this might arouse suspicion. Ruby Redfort says: If you are trying to avoid arousing suspicion then you must act NORMAL.

Acting normal means **not** talking about **turkeys**
and **how much** one might **cost**.
So I will do exactly as Ruby says:
RULE #1: KEEP IT ZIPPED
i.e. keep your trap shut.
When I finally come out and take a proper look
around, I notice that the floor is **very shiny** and
there is **no sign** of a **turkey**.

Not anywhere.
I can't see it in the kitchen fridge or the shed fridge
and I am **utterly lost for ideas** of where it could
have got to.
Granny often says 'dwelling on **things**
you **can't fix** can make you **very unhappy**'
and 'sometimes **it's best** to

put problems **behind** you'
so this is what I do.
It is very **good advice** because no one says
a word about the **missing bird**.
Mum asks if I made Mrs Rippon a cup of tea
and I do a **sneeze** and say *yes*.
She LOOKS at me with **suspicious eyes** but she
DOESN'T say ANYTHING.

So **perhaps** everything's going to
turn out well
after all.

NINE

Sing Choirs of Angels

AT FIVE O'CLOCK IT IS TIME TO PUT ON coats and get going. I am travelling to the school carol concert with the Moodys.

Call-me–Cecil is taking us because he also has to be there early as a performer and me and Betty have to be there early to do our warming-ups. Everyone is actually very excited except for Robert Granger who has forgotten his silver cape. Luckily, Mrs Singh has brought a spare one along so the whole thing is NOT ruined.

When it gets to five minutes to six o'clock we all have to be quiet and shuffle on to the stage. All the audience is there and sitting on chairs without talking and the Julia Moggan Hall is all in the dark with NO lights, just candles and . . .

an exceptionOrdinarily
BIG Christmas tree,
even bigger than our one.

Mrs Wilberton won't trust children with real candles, so we have to use those plastic ones that pretend to flicker but are battery-powered. I think plastic candles aren't really the spirit of Christmas but the people in the audience don't seem to mind and are carried away by the singing. I am standing next to Karl Wrenbury and Toby Hawkling, who I can tell you aren't singing the correct words but luckily no one can hear or they would be put outside with their coats on. When it gets to 'The Twelve Days of Christmas' Mrs Wilberton looks pinched in the face. This is due to my cousin Noah, who is meant to be the partridge in the pear tree but is instead *wilting* on a chair. He looks like he already has car sickness and it is probably just the thought of the nine hours' drive to see the Robertseses on Christmas Eve which has made him want to vomit. Thoughts definitely can have a BAD effect.

You can hear the fidgeting in the audience
because there is a gap between the singing that
is NOT meant to be there, and I can tell
Mrs Wilberton is beginning to PANIC.
Mrs Wilberton says,

'We need a NEW partridge
in a pear tree, *quick sticks!*'

I put my hand up.
She is squawking in a wobbly voice and says,
'Any volunteers who know the part!'
And I shout, 'ME!'
But even though she is looking right at
me she doesn't seem to see me and
I am utterly ignored.
In the end it is decided that I will
not be swapped in at the last minute
but Audrey Broadley will. At first she
is really good but halfway through she
does get muddled up with the various
numbers of birds and Mrs Wilberton
goes very *HARSH* in the eyes
and if I were Audrey Broadley I would
NOT stay for the mince pies.

Right at the very end the **pretend pear** falls off
the tree and **rolls** across the stage and this puts
Audrey into a T R A N C E and she **forgets**
to **sing** the last *'partridge in a pear tree'*
and the song **can't** finish
without that and everyone
is **waiting**

> and waiting

so I sing it

because someone has to.
And Peggy stands up and
starts **clapping** and
everyone stands up
and starts **clapping**
and Grace Grapello
says, 'I didn't **know** you
had such a **good voice**,
Clarice Bean,'
and I say, 'Thank you,
Grace. That's **very nice**
of you to say,' which it is.

Afterwards, when the lights are turned up and we've all got down off the stage,

Peggy says,

'Clarice Bean, you sing like an angel.'

Dad says, 'You didn't tell us you had a solo part,' and Mum says, 'Yes, that was a

wonderful surprise,'

and call-me-Cecil just winks.

Then there is a lot of chatting and Peggy says she's going off to find Mrs Wilberton and Grandad says,

'I wouldn't want to be in *her* shoes.'

People are allowed ONE mince pie per person and a hot drink out of a plastic cup. Due to environmental reasons and my mum and dad promising Kurt not to drink out of plastic cups they have to go thirsty. Dad has a choking episode with a pie that is rather dry, and he has to *rush off* to find a tap.

Marguerite, Al and Noah say they have to *rush* back to the babysitter who is at home with cousin Yolla.

Dad tries to persuade them to pop in for some
Christmas soup but they say,
'We have such an early start in the morning
        that we must get straight to bed.'
Mum says, 'Make sure you ring us when you
get to the Robertses,'
and they say, 'We certainly will!' and we all
have to wish them Merry Christmas in a hurry
and this is sad because we won't see them until
it is all over. Even sadder is that I can't give Betty
her Christmas present and it was specially
bought for the plane trip.
Betty says, 'It doesn't matter, Clarice Bean.
It will be something to look forward to.'
Call-me-Mol says, 'I know what we'll do –
as soon as we get back, you can all come over
for new year!'
This cheers us up like anything and we arrive
home in a very good mood and discover Mum
has put decorations up and down the stairs
and in the hall.
She says never forget the hall because that is
the most important place to have good cheer

and welcome people
to our home.

Unfortunately Cement has had a terrible episode
of the vomits all over the cleaned floor,
and Dad says, 'Well, that's a nice welcome home,'
and Mum says, 'Whatever is the matter
with that dog?'
and Grandad says, 'I think he swallowed some
filthy puddle water in the park.'
But even Dad cleaning something unpleasant off
the floor cannot cause us to lose the good spirits
we are all in.
Mum has made a very nice dinner, which is a
purple soup and a baked potato.
She says, 'Minal has kindly decorated the table.'
For some reason Minal has chosen to make his
decorations spiders but I decide NOT to make
a comment about this because I don't think this
would be in the Christmas spirit even though
spiders definitely AREN'T anything to do
with Christmas.
Things are going very well and it is even agreed
that we might play Sevens after dinner. Sevens
is a card game and everyone in my family likes
playing cards and this includes us ALL.

But then the Christmas spirit is interrupted.
Because Minal *knocks* his drink into Marcie's
pudding and she is tipped over the edge.
This makes Kurt aggravated and he says she is
overreacting as usual.
She says, 'Well, at least I *can* react and don't just
sit there like a potato.'
He says something very RUDE to Marcie,
which is NOT at-the-table language.
And Dad says, 'That is not at-the-table language.'
And I say, 'Could I—'
And Dad says, 'Do NOT repeat it, Clarice Bean!'
And Marcie says, 'Yes, stay out of it.'
I say, 'I was only going to ask for the sugar,'
and Mum says, 'I don't think this pudding needs
more sugar, doesn't everyone agree?'
She is trying to change the subject.
But Marcie says, 'Well, I wouldn't know
because my pudding is underwater.'
Minal says, 'It's just a *spilt* drink!'
She says, 'OK, so you eat it, squirt!'
So he does and Marcie screeches.
I say, 'Don't get your underwear in a bunch.'

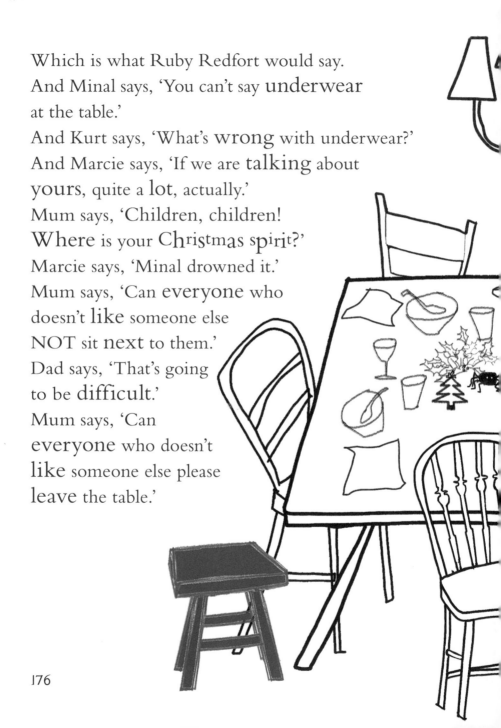

Which is what Ruby Redfort would say.
And Minal says, 'You can't say underwear
at the table.'
And Kurt says, 'What's wrong with underwear?'
And Marcie says, 'If we are talking about
yours, quite a lot, actually.'
Mum says, 'Children, children!
Where is your Christmas spirit?'
Marcie says, 'Minal drowned it.'
Mum says, 'Can everyone who
doesn't like someone else
NOT sit next to them.'
Dad says, 'That's going
to be difficult.'
Mum says, 'Can
everyone who doesn't
like someone else please
leave the table.'

Grandad is left sitting
on his own.

Mum goes off to have some time to herself
in the bath.
Dad says he is going to stand at the bottom of
the garden for a while.
Everybody else goes to their own room
        and I climb into the airing cupboard.

Everything
is wrong.

The Christmas spirit has gone missing.
And when I go downstairs to get a glass of water
I find the Advent candle has
        burned down to the end.

It's definitely
NOT
going to
snow
now.

TEN

⁊In the Bleak Midwinter

ON CHRISTMAS EVE I GET UP EARLY.
Getting up early is not normal for me but
Christmas Eve is different from all the other days
and I never want to waste even a minute.
This year I can't *afford* to waste even a *second*
because I'm really behind with everything due
to being locked up in the toilet when I should have
been finishing my Christmas-present preparations,
i.e. writing my gift tags. I run upstairs to ask Mum
if I may use the kitchen in privatude but I am not
allowed to actually peep in the door because she
is wrapping presents in the TINY study whilst
talking to Granny on the speakerphone.

10

Do **NOT**
come in

Please
STOP sticking
STICKERS on
THIS door.

I hear Granny say, 'Yes, your Christmas parcel arrived. It's huge – I had to get the janitor to help me take it up to my apartment.'
Mum says, 'What do you mean huge?'
She sounds like she has a funny look on her face like she's trying to puzzle something out which cannot be puzzled. It is beginning to dawn on me that Mr Felixstow might at this very moment be wondering what to do with a TINY-USEFUL-THINGS BAG and a macaroni necklace.
So I tiptoe in the other direction and look for Dad instead.
This takes at least twelve minutes because he is not in his usual place and is in fact down the garden trying to stop a fence blowing away. When I tell him my plan he asks if 'using the kitchen will involve heat and or sharp implements?'.
And of course it does because this is what a kitchen is mainly for.
He says I will need responsible supervision and he can't help because he's having trouble with the wind.

I explain how I *would* normally suggest Betty
since she is the most responsible person I know
but she is about to be off to Japan.
And Dad says,
'I agree. Betty Moody would have been
            a good choice as she is indeed one of
the most responsible people any of us know,
        certainly more responsible than most
of the people I work with but, in any case, it
needs to be someone of at least sixteen or over.'
So I choose Grandad because he is the one most
likely to forget what we are doing and the only
other person more than the age of a teenager.
Grandad says yes because of course he always
does, even though he is busy doing a jigsaw puzzle
on the coffee table. Lots of pieces have fallen on
the floor, and I hope he finds them before Cement
eats them.
I say, 'Grandad, don't look at the name of what
we are making, just only the recipe.'
He says, 'Boiled sugar with vanilla, milk and
butter. Sounds delicious.' Then he says,
'I think we should wear pinnies.'

In the end we decide we should also wear **swimming goggles** just to be on the safer side, because, you see, sugar **boils at 102.82 degrees** centigrade. I learned that from my science project. **Fudge sounds dangerous.**

To begin with you must put all your ingredients in a row and find the cooking scales, which are **not** in the cupboard where your mum said they were and are **actually** in her bedroom where she has been **weighing parcels** for the post office.

Making **fudge is easy** and **also** hard. It is not hard to do the recipe, which is mainly **melting** things together, but it *is* **hard** to make the fudge **fudge-ish**.

I don't think mine has turned into
what it is meant to turn into.
It is not crumbly and there is
nothing soft about it and
it has actually turned into
a disappointment.
Grandad says,
'I am certain
that – whatever
this is meant to
be – it is NOT a
disappointment.'
It is nice of him
to say this, but
I don't think
it's true since
I have to chop
it up with a
hammer, which
is NOT something
you normally
need to do
with fudge.

★ ★ ★

By lunchtime Dad is just preparing to go to the shops and start his Christmas shopping. He says having only four hours to get it done concentrates the mind. Minal is making more macaroni jewellery and I go off to my room to write my gift tags. On my way past the front door I find a puffy envelope addressed to me. I open it and there is Betty Moody's Christmas present, the one I sent off for, but sadly it is too late because she is by now on her way to the airport. I take it up to my room and unwrap it and I realise that it is even better than I thought it was and most definitely worth the special offer of £7.99 and it is just what Betty would need on an eleven-and-a-half-hour flight to Tokyo. I am wondering which gift tag Betty would like most – probably an elf on a toadstool – when I hear Mum calling up the stairs in a stretched voice,

'Does anyone know what has happened to the turkey? It is NOT in the shed fridge.'

And of course I am FROZEN with panic so I go
a bit quiet and pretend I haven't heard her.
And Mum shouts, 'Marcie? MARCIE!
MARCIE! Have YOU seen the turkey?'
Marcie: 'What turkey?'
Mum: 'What do you mean "*what* turkey"?
The Christmas turkey.
Do you know where it has got to?'
Marcie: 'No.'
Mum: 'Kurt?'
Kurt: 'Why would I know what has happened
to the turkey? I'm a vegetarian.'

Pause.

Mum: 'Minal, have you seen the turkey?'
Minal: 'Yes.'
Mum: 'Where is it?'
Minal: 'I don't know.'
Mum: 'When did you *last* see it?'
Minal: 'When it was on the floor.'
Mum: 'What!'
Minal: 'On the floor.'

Mum: 'What was it doing on the floor?'

Minal: 'It was being eaten by Cement.'

Mum: 'Cement ate the whole turkey?'

Minal: 'No, the fox ate half.'

Mum: 'What fox?'

Minal: 'The one who comes into the kitchen.'

Mum: 'Minal, can we please return to planet Earth for two minutes!'

Minal: 'But . . .'

Mum: 'When did you see a turkey on the floor?'

Minal: 'Yesterday when Clarice was locked in the toilet and, by the way, she nibbled the lemon drizzle cake.'

Silence.

And then . . .

'Clarice Bean!'

But I have already climbed inside the
airing cupboard and am closing the door

and hardly
    taking
        a
        b r e a t h.

ELEVEN

It's Beginning to Look a Lot Like Christmas

I AM JUST WORRYING IF I WILL EVER BE able to come out when Kurt peeks in and says, 'The coast is clear.'

I say, 'How did you know I was in *here*?'

and he says, 'This is where you always go when you are in trouble.'

Marcie says, 'Don't worry, Clarice.
They'll get over it.'

Kurt says, 'They'll forget about it.'

I say, 'They won't forget they have a turkey eaten by a dog.'

Minal says, 'You do know Father Christmas isn't going to leave you any presents.'

Marcie says, 'MINAL!'

and Minal says, 'But it's TRUE,

if you're bad he doesn't come.'
Kurt says, 'That's rubbish.'
  But I know that it's NOT rubbish – it is
    a well-known FACT.
Marcie says, 'I'll ring Granny. She always has
good ideas for getting out of tricky situations.'
And so Marcie telephones Granny and explains
about the turkey trouble.
And Granny says, 'Where is your mother now?'
and Marcie tells her how Mum has had to rush out
of the house without a second thought because
there has been an emergency due to the storm.
And the emergency is a tree which has fallen on
the roof of Uncle Ted and JoJo's flat and now
for their own complete safety they are NOT
allowed to be there having Christmas for two.
              And, just like Marcie said she would,
                    Granny has a good idea.
                        And this is it:

So that's what we decide to do:

> Tidy up.
> Lay the table.
> Make dinner.
> And most of all say **sorry**.

And then we all get tidying.
And when we have finished tidying we lay the table.
By the time we have finished you would
think the elves had been over.
We are very pleased with ourselves until Marcie
says, 'But what about dinner?'

Everybody is a BLANK because nobody knows
what the answer is. Then Grandad comes in
through the front door with Cement.
They are very *windblown* with their hair off
in the wrong direction.
Grandad says, 'We just bumped into our friend Karl
and he gave us this envelope – it's for you, Clarice.'
It is all decorated in Christmas stickers and it says
in Karl's writing: **Open now or save until later.**

So I open now. Inside there is a very neatly written-out recipe and a note from Karl that says:

Mrs Tomassini taught me how to make this dinner and I bet you could make it too! Happy Christmas Clarice Bean

from Karl

PS it is really good

One thing I'm sure about is that we do have the main ingredient. And now I utterly know what to make for dinner.

At seventeen minutes past six Mum comes
home with Dad who has arrived back with
NO presents but, instead, Uncle Ted and JoJo.
They all look very tired.
   But they perk up when Uncle Ted says,
      'What's cooking?'

and JoJo says, 'Oh, wow, that smells so amazing.'
Mum says, 'Is that *dinner*?'
and Minal says, 'It's macaroni!'
and I say, 'Cheese.'
Dad says, 'Did the elves visit while we were gone?'
and Mum says, 'I don't remember the house EVER being this tidy,'
and JoJo says, 'You've gone M I N I M A L I S T.'
Mum says, 'Yes, where's ALL the clutter?'
and Marcie says, 'We put it in the shed.'
Grandad says, 'Where's my puzzle?'
Minal says, 'I vacuumed it up!'
and Kurt says,

    'Dinner is served.'

And then we all sit down and I spoon out the
macaroni cheese, which everybody agrees is
exceptionOrdinarily better than any other kind
of macaroni cheese because it has a twist and
the twist is vegetables.

JoJo says, 'I can't believe you cooked this
yourselves.'

Marcie says, 'It was mainly Clarice.'

I say, 'Everyone helped.'

Mum says, 'I'm so glad you found a USE for
ALL that macaroni,'

and Dad says, 'Yes, who knew you could
actually eat it.'

Uncle Ted says, 'I hope lunch tomorrow will be
this delicious.'

Mum says, 'Ah, yes, that's the GOOD news:
Ted and JoJo will be staying for Christmas,'

and JoJo says, 'It's SO generous of you
to share your Christmas with US.'

Mum: 'But of course –
          that's what Christmas is about.'

Dad: 'And we have plenty to share.
I accidentally ordered a much–too–big turkey.'

Mum: 'Ah, that's the BAD news.'

Dad: 'What do you mean the BAD news?'

And I say,

'The bad news is *my* fault because you told me
NOT to put it in the kitchen fridge
or there would be chaos
and there WAS chaos.'

Dad: 'Could someone explain?'

Kurt: 'It was all my fault for not putting it in the shed like you asked.'

Dad: 'Are we talking turkey?'

Marcie: 'It's probably Cement's fault –
he's the one who ate it.'

Uncle Ted: 'Cement ate the turkey?'

Minal: 'And was sick on the floor.'

Grandad: 'Oh dear – it's probably my fault for allowing Cement to eat from the table.'

Marcie: 'Cement wasn't eating from the table.'

Grandad: 'He opened the fridge?'

Kurt: 'It was on the floor.'

Minal: 'The fox ate most of it.'

JoJo: 'You keep a fox?'

Grandad: 'I'm confused.'

Mum: 'Minal, would you please STOP talking about the imaginary fox!'
and I say, 'Sorry, because it was
                            actually ALL my fault,'
and Kurt says,
        'Sorry, because it was also MY fault,'
and Grandad says,
        'Sorry because Cement should know better than to eat turkeys dropped on the floor,'
and Mum says, 'Never mind.'
Dad says, 'If a missing turkey can have everyone in such agreement then I am glad Cement ate it . . . I wish he hadn't been sick on the floor but it's a SMALL price to pay for a happy household.'
Even without the Advent candle you can tell it is going to be Christmas Day tomorrow because the Christmas spirit has utterly returned and it is interesting that everyone has gone back to being more like their Christmas selves now we are nine.
It is beginning to feel a lot like Christmas.
Mum gets up and peers into the larder. She says, 'I wonder what we will eat for lunch tomorrow?'
and Dad says, 'Something potatoey I should think.'

I say, 'It's a shame Marguerite isn't coming.
She is a very inventive cook.'
We listen to the wind *whistling* round the house
and the tree tapping at the window and Mum
says, 'I do hope they all arrived safely with the
Robertses – it's not nice weather to be driving in.'
Dad says, 'Nine hours is a long time to be in a car.'
Grandad says, 'It's very chilly out.
I hope they've taken their warm socks.'
Mum looks distracted and says,
'Where are Ted and JoJo going to sleep?'
Kurt says, 'They can have my room – I can
sleep on the floor of the TINY study,'
and everyone smiles.
Except for Dad who goes to fetch the yellow
rubber gloves and the air freshener.
My brother's room is a danger to germs.

★ ★ ★

While everyone is moving things from one place
to another and freshening up Kurt's bedroom,
I go and finish work on my Christmas presents.

Luckily, I have made so much fudge there is plenty for Uncle Ted and JoJo with quite a lot left over for emergencies. Once I have popped it into the paper heart decorations and attached my gift tags, I hang them all on the tree. Grandad says it looks very eye-catching and I think I agree. This is the successful bit and so long as no one tries to eat it, it will be a good present.

After everything has been completely done, we all sit down to watch the film of Mary Poppins. Even Kurt watches and no one complains at all. Then we put our stockings on the end of the beds and turn out the light and try our best to go to sleep even though some of us are still chatting downstairs and keeping other people awake.

It is hard to go to sleep because how can you get your heart to stop beating so much and your mind to stop wishing for the morning? And the more you want to sleep the more you can't.

I am almost on the very edge of *drifting* off when I seem to hear a piano and my ears stand up on end and I wait and I think I am definitely listening to tuneful notes.

And so I tiptoe downstairs
in the absolute dark.
And only the Christmas tree
lights are awake.

And I peek into the living room and my eyes
adjust to the twinkling gloom,
and next to the fireplace there is the eaten
minced pie and the drunk drink ALL gone.
And it can only be you-know-who has been
down the chimney.
So I quietly creep back up to my bed and I listen
to the storm and think about how the wind
blows Mary Poppins to the door.

And I wish it could do the same for us –
    I wish the wind could *blow*
        more people to *our* door.

And I wish it could bring the snow.
    I wish it could.

        And just before I fall
            into my dreams . . .

I am sure I can hear the sound
of whispering elves
playing a piano.

TWELVE

Have Yourself a Merry Little Christmas

I WAKE UP AND WE ALL WAKE UP, AND this is what happens.

With my toes I can feel something heavy on the end of my bed and straight away I know two things.

ONE: Father Christmas and the elves have definitely been.

TWO: There is NOT a piano in my stocking.

My eyes are only slightly adjusted to the morning since it is 6:22 on the alarm clock and so it takes me a few milliseconds to realise that my bedroom is FULL of cousins. Yolla and Noah are standing there readily dressed for Christmas in their Christmas presents. I am astonished of course.

Minal says, 'How are you here
when you are at the Robertseses?'

and Noah says, 'Because we didn't GO,'

and Yolla says, 'NO, we aren't there.'

We all open my stocking fillers and even though
there isn't even one thing from on my list I can
see that actually Father Christmas has had some
good ideas of his own.

For instance, e.g., a TINY tape-measure keyring
which I know for a fact he got from the post-
office-convenient store – it still has
the price tag on it.

So I suppose it DOES make sense that he buys
his wrapping paper from there too.

We all go down for breakfast
where most people are
eating eggs in pyjamas.

Marguerite says,
'You see, Clarice Bean,
your wish came true!'

I say, 'Oh, did the
Robertseses get infectious
tummy bugs?'

Al says, 'Not as far as I know.
The problem is our car – it's

suffering from old age. It wouldn't start because the weather's too cold,' and Marguerite says, 'I didn't like the look of it at all – it's getting icy.'

They all look really pleased.

Mum says, 'Just imagine if it had snowed and you'd got stuck in the middle of nowhere?'

And then I look really pleased.

Dad says, 'It's not going to snow.'

Minal eats too many jellybeans and has started running round and round the kitchen so Mum

puts a hat on him and makes him run round and round the garden twenty-seven times. It's quite funny to watch and Noah takes several pictures with his instant camera, which came in his stocking. Al says that Noah and Yolla opened ALL their presents

at five o'clock in the morning, and this
makes me think about Grandad because he is
usually an early riser but where is he?
Uncle Ted says, 'He's popped over to Peggy's to
wish her and her family a happy Christmas.'
Mum says, 'She is going to be so busy.

    There are thirteen of them, you know.'
I say, 'The same as us.' Since with the added
cousins and uncle and aunt we are now thirteen.
Dad says, 'Lucky for some.'
Once we've had breakfast Mum starts rummaging
in the larder to see what we can have for Christmas
dinner now the main part of it has been eaten by
a dog. We are all adapting to a vegetable-only
lunch and probably spaghetti when Grandad
comes home with Peggy.
Mum says, 'Peggy! We are so happy to see you!'
and Marguerite says, 'Are your family outside?'
and Peggy says, 'It's a long story!'
Which actually it isn't because they are just stuck
at abroad airports due to stormy conditions and the
planes not being allowed up. So no one at all is
coming until at least tomorrow.

Dad says, 'Will you join us for spaghetti and sprouts?'
and Peggy says, 'Close your eyes and make a wish.'

And when we open them there is a

HUGE turkey

on the table.

Peggy say, 'Happy Christmas, one and all!'
Noah says, 'Where did THAT come from?'
and Peggy says, 'My kitchen.'
Dad says, 'You didn't *carry* it all the way here,
did you?'
and Peggy says, 'No, I used an old shopping
trolley that was parked outside my house.'
She says, 'It was like an angel left it there
for just this very reason.'
And now, just like that, we are fourteen.
It means lunch will become dinner because
GIANT turkeys take a lot of time to cook,
and Dad says it might be a good idea if some of us
go out for a run around. He is mainly looking
at Minal, who is still very hyperly-active from
the jellybeans.

So most of us go for a walk up the hill
and we meet Karl and Alf
   and we climb up the trees
      and we *race* around the wood
and we are gone ages even though it is cold
and we almost turn blue in the toes
and no one wants to STOP.
But in the end we have to,
so we say goodbye to Karl and Alf
            and walk back
               down
                  the
                     hill.

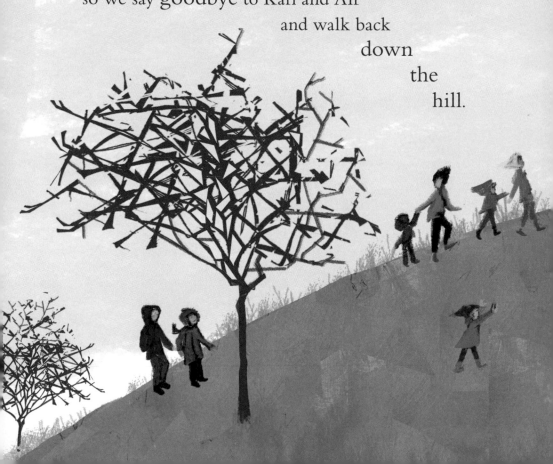

When we turn the corner
we see Dad is waiting
at the top of our street
wondering
where
we are.

By the time we get home everyone
is really quite exceptionordinarily
hungry and nearly perished to ice.

Mum has lit all the candles
and the house looks like one of those
old-fashioned paintings
from the past.

We all sit down and we are just about
to start eating when Peggy says,
'Do you hear that?'
And Mum says, 'Yes, I think I do.'
Minal says, 'Is it a FOX?'
JoJo says, 'I think it's singing.'
Yolla says, 'A singing fox?'
Marcie says, 'Carol singers.'
Kurt says, 'Where is it coming from?'
Uncle Ted says, 'Outside the door,'
and Dad says,
'Clarice, go and have a look.'

And so I do.

It is already dark but I can see four people
and a dog standing on the doorstep singing,
   and the song is
      'We Wish You a Merry Christmas'
and the dog is Pekinese and it is wearing
a choirboy costume.
And the amazing thing is it's all of the Moodys
on our actual doorstep.
            And they all say,

'Merry Christmas, Clarice Bean!'

I say, 'How are you here when you are on the
plane to Japan?'
and Betty says, 'Your mum called us
      because she thought we might be stuck at
            the airport due to wind.'
Call-me-Mol says, 'I hope you don't mind us
      bringing Ralph? We borrowed him back
            from the neighbours.'
Grandad says, 'Cement will be pleased.'

And now, just like that, we are nineteen if you
count Ralph, but since he is dressed as a boy I do.

It is a Squash . . .

but we all **squish** round the table
and everyone fits **exactly**.

★ ★ ★

After dinner I give out my fudge which is enough for
one each and Peggy says it is more like old-fashioned
toffee, and toffee in her opinion is even nicer than
fudge, even if you do have to chop it up with a
hammer. Minal is NOT allowed to eat his until
tomorrow in case it sets him off again because,
you see, there is not enough room to have a boy
running around the kitchen.

Betty is very pleased with the **RUBY REDFORT
FLY LIGHT** and it is passed around the room
and Grandad says he will put it on his Christmas
list for next year.

And *everyone* is very pleased with all their presents
including me and so I am utterly surprised when
Mum says,

   'Oh, we almost forgot, Father Christmas left
      THIS one here last night – it's for YOU.'

And Uncle Ted jumps up, and Dad jumps up
and they help slowly *DRAG* the Christmas tree
away from the wall until I can see a large shape
through the branches.

Dad says, 'I guess it wouldn't **squeeze** into a stocking.'

And I realise Betty Moody was right.
I have NOT been believing in NOTHING
after all – I just needed to use a stamp.
And I say,
    'I *knew* I could hear the elves
          playing the piano last night.'
And Betty whispers, 'You see, Clarice Bean,
you didn't even need a back-up plan.'
Call-me-Cecil sits down on the little stool
and says, 'So what shall we sing?'
and I say, 'How about *"Let it Snow"*?'
And we sing and sing
and everyone stays up very, very late
without getting tired and we play Charades
and the drawing game and cards
until it is time for the Moodys and Peggy and
the cousins to leave and although we are sorry
to see them go when we open the door
    to wave them goodbye
        you will not believe it
    because it is the kind of thing
        which only happens in the books
          or in the films.

Because   you see . . .

it is   really properly snowing.

The End of Things

We called granny very late on Christmas evening to tell her that it had been quite an unexpected day of exactly what it was supposed to be.

And even though there were 114 potatoes to peel nobody flumped in a chair with tiredness and that's because nineteen people, which includes a choirboy dog, is always the right number for Christmas.

Granny said she was very pleased with all the old jumpers. It is NOT what she was expecting and she has a feeling that it is NOT what Mum had expected to be sending her, but it couldn't be more suitable, because she and her friend Wallace

are planning to do some mending and
set up a stall selling reconditioned knitwear.
     She said she will mend my cardigans
                  and send them right back to me.

Mum looked at me and said,
     'I wonder how Mr Felixstow is getting on
with his parcel,' and then she explained to Granny
about the mix-up and Granny said,
     'I am sure he will be very comfortable in
my new slippers, but the prescription sunglasses
                  may give him eye-ache.'

Mum said, 'He must think we've gone a bit mad.
     What's he going to do with ALL those
                  peculiar presents?'

Dad said, 'He can always cook the macaroni necklace.'

And Grandad said, 'I think Mr Felixstow will wonder how he ever managed without a TINY-USEFUL-THINGS BAG.'

And Granny said, 'Exactly.'

I told her I would make her another one and she said she would look forward to it and she hoped the **RUBY REDFORT LONG-DISTANCE WALKIE-TALKIES** might arrive in time for my birthday.

And I said I would look forward to that and then we all said goodbye.

And now it is time to go up to bed and even though I don't want it to be over my eyes are beginning to fall asleep without me.

But while I am slowly climbing the stairs I think about the day and even though I didn't get the fish or the tank it doesn't matter, because I can put them on my list for next Christmas.

Minal gave me the fish food, which was really very thoughtful, and it doesn't go off for another six years, so I have plenty of time.

Just before I climb into bed, I tiptoe over to the
window and look out at the snowflakes falling,
and I can hear Uncle Ted playing the piano
and he is singing a song about the snow and
the words carry me away and remind me of my
Advent-candle wish and how it came true –
and it's just like Ruby Redfort says,

'How can your wishes come TRUE,
if you NEVER even bother to wish?'

Then I tuck into bed,
close my eyes
and
drift
into
dreams.

'Oh my goodness, there's a fox in the kitchen.'

'I told you there was!'

Christmas songs adapted by Clarice Bean

**CHRISTMAS IS COMING
THE GOOSE IS GETTING FAT**
'Christmas is Coming'
traditional nursery rhyme and song, first set to music in 1800s

GLAD TIDINGS OF GREAT JOY
'While Shepherds Watched their Flocks by Night'
traditional carol from around 1700

JOY TO THE WORLD
'Joy to the World'
Christmas carol by Isaac Watts, 1719

**CHRISTMAS TREE
OH CHRISTMAS TREE**
'O Christmas Tree'
traditional German carol, 1500s

SING CHOIRS OF ANGELS
'O Come all Ye Faithful'
traditional carol from around 1744

IN THE BLEAK MIDWINTER
'In the Bleak Midwinter'
based on the poem by Christina Rossetti, 1872

**IT'S BEGINNING TO LOOK
A LOT LIKE CHRISTMAS**
'It's Beginning to Look a Lot Like Christmas'
by Meredith Wilson, 1951

**HAVE YOURSELF A MERRY
LITTLE CHRISTMAS**
'Have Yourself a Merry Little Christmas'
by Hugh Martin and Ralph Blane, 1943

**GOODWILL
TO ALL PEOPLEKIND**
'It Came Upon a Midnight Clear'
based on the poem by Edmund Sears, 1849

HARK HEAR THE BELLS
'Carol of the Bells'
Christmas carol from 1914

MERRILY ON HIGH
'Ding Dong Merrily on High'
Christmas carol from around 1924

**DECK THE HALLS
WITH BOUGHS OF HOLLY**
'Deck the Halls'
traditional carol, 1500s

More exceptionOrdinarily good books
by Lauren Child

I would like to thank the following for all their talent, support and inspiration:

Rachel Folder, Goldy Broad, Lydia Barram, Sam Stewart, Val Brathwaite, KB and David Mackintosh.

Tuesday Child for the Advent calendar drawing
and for baking the lemon drizzle cake.

Mini Steward for writing the numbers and
Bibi Steward for making the paper heart basket.

Special thanks as always to AJM,
and of course to AD for his unerring support.

First
published in
Great Britain by
HarperCollins *Children's Books* in 2021
HarperCollins *Children's Books*
is a division of HarperCollins*Publishers* Ltd,
1 London Bridge Street, London SE1 9GF
www.harpercollins.co.uk
HarperCollins*Publishers*
1st Floor, Watermarque Building, Ringsend Road, Dublin 4, Ireland
1
Text and illustrations copyright © Lauren Child 2021
Cover design copyright © HarperCollins*Publishers* Ltd 2021
All rights reserved.
ISBN 978-0-00-847084-5
Lauren Child asserts the moral right to be
identified as the author and illustrator of the work respectively.
A CIP catalogue record for this title is available from the British Library.
Designed by Goldy Broad
Printed and bound in Bosnia and Herzegovina by GPS Group
Conditions of Sale
This book is sold subject to the condition that it shall not, by way of trade or otherwise,
be lent, re-sold, hired out or otherwise circulated without the publisher's prior consent in any form,
binding or cover other than that in which it is published and without a similar condition including this condition being
imposed on the subsequent purchaser.
Find
out
more
about
HarperCollins
and the environment at
www.harpercollins.co.uk/green

Thanks to Hachette Children's Books for use of the Clarice Bean series lettering